AMERICA'S MOST WANTED SHORT STORIES

AMERICA'S MOST WANTED SHORT STORIES

"We Have Just Begun To Write"

Mike & Veronica Krath

Copyright © 2000 by Mike & Veronica Krath.

Library of Congress Number: 00-191343
ISBN #:   Softcover   0-7388-2612-X

All rights reserved. No part of this book may be reproduced or transmitted in any form or by any means, electronic or mechanical, including photocopying, recording, or by any information storage and retrieval system, without permission in writing from the copyright owner.

This is a work of fiction. Names, characters, places and incidents either are the product of the author's imagination or are used fictitiously, and any resemblance to any actual persons, living or dead, events, or locales is entirely coincidental.

This book was printed in the United States of America.

To order additional copies of this book, contact:
Xlibris Corporation
1-888-7-XLIBRIS
www.Xlibris.com
Orders@Xlibris.com

CONTENTS

Foreword 9

Meteor Rex 11
Fund Day 15
Jumping Jim 17
Disposable Art 23
Welcome to the Family 27
Jo Lena 36
A Spring Love Story 44
The Lost Christmas Party 62
A Walk in the Woods 65
The Dinner Date 77
Family Vacation 84
Goodbye, Robert 92
Chara, Girl of the Eighties and into the Nineties! 98
The Magic Show 104
Mrs. Monkey 107
The Groovy Date 108
The Office Barter System 111
World Court 114
My First Alien Encounter 116
A Fund Experiment 120
Happy Chinese New Year! 124
Fred's Psycho Wife's Luncheon 128
Christmas Candle 131
Jim and the Book 134

Movie Time	136
The Camera Story	140
Pink, Fluffy Clouds	142
Pedro's Surprise	145
How We Obtained Our Rabbit Skin Rug, or Why Animals are Extinct	146
Writer's Block!	148
New York	152
The Language Tutor	153
The Newlyweds	156
The Lovely Bride	157
The New Computer	162
The Kiss	163
No Ghost of a Chance!	170
Punishment	173
Final Thoughts and Conversations of the Tenants Prior to the Collapse of Their 25th Story Building	177
David the Easter Bunny	180
No Time for Siesta!	183
The Perfect Mother—a short, short summary of perfection	188
The Love Birds	190
Appendix	197

To Owen, Jonathan, Rebecca, Matthew, Elizabeth and Mary

FOREWORD

My wife and I enjoy writing stories to entertain each other. I will start a story and call my wife to come and add a few paragraphs. After she does, I sit down and write a few more. You might say this is a good way to get rid of writer's block. You might also say that this is a good reason our stories end up the way they do.

Most of our stories deal with romantic issues. The couples are slightly deranged. Some of them begin the story acting quite normal and then get hit on the head by a falling brick or roof or whatever we find appropriate. This is how we do our character change—albeit, always for the worse.

We have been writing together for almost thirty years. We met at Cairo American College, an American High School in Cairo, Egypt while sophomores. We found then, as we do now, that trying to help ruin each other's stories was a source of great pride and joy.

You might say the creativity and humor exercised back then was the main reason for us becoming friends, then close friends, and finally married friends with six children and two cats.

With such an abundant life, we find the creativity and humor never cease.

God Bless.

Mike and Veronica Krath
Fort Worth, Texas 2000

METEOR REX

He told about everyone in the office. Frank hadn't heard the story, but when Joe began to tell him, even though Frank wasn't interested, he feigned interest to impress Joe that he was such a great listener. First, Frank just grinned. Then he decided he would be more impressive by just opening his mouth in mock surprise. Joe started to lose his own attention in telling his story since Frank was acting so weird.

"Do you still want me to continue with my story?" Joe suddenly asked.

Frank was taken aback by the remark. Wasn't he playing the role of an interested listener?

"Why, Joe, of course, I want you to continue," Frank said, acting as if Joe were crazy not to continue.

Joe began where he had left off, and Frank sat solemn, staring into space. He decided he shouldn't do anything now since Joe was not pleased with grins and opened gapes.

When Joe got to his punch line and started laughing, Frank just sat still, moribund, arms crossed, stoic, a statue of angst never cracking a smile, eyes bulging and listless. Joe immediately stopped laughing and started to stare at Frank.

"What's your problem, Frank?" Joe said.

"It's coming right at us!" Frank screamed.

"What? What's wrong, Frank?" Joe asked.

At that very moment, on a collision course to a great spheroid called Planet Earth, spinning on its axis and orbiting the sun, ninety million miles from its helical flames, a meteor of immense proportions was increasing its speed.

Pat was quite happy with his story. He read it over and over again and congratulated himself. The only other thing was to make it into a stage play. He had read about an outfit in the paper that would take your story and turn it into a Broadway quality type play—and all for ten thousand dollars!

"I have always wanted to have a play on Broadway," Pat said.

Pat withdrew ten thousand from his IRA's, paying a hefty pre-withdrawal penalty, and sent it, along with a copy of his story, to the Jim Bob Playwright Company.

Several weeks went past, and Pat received a letter in the mail. It said: Your play is in the mail

"My play! My Broadway play is coming!" Pat said and jumped up and down for joy.

He threw a lavish party for all his friends—taking out another $10,000 from his IRA funds and once again paying a hefty early pre-withdrawal penalty.

The next day, Pat received his play in the mail with a note:

"If this doesn't meet with your 100% satisfaction, please call for a complete refund."

Pat began eagerly to read his play:

METEOR
DRAMATIS PERSONÆ
FRANK, Interested Listener
SIR OLIVER MARTEXT, a Vicar.
JOE, Brother to the DUKE, and Usurper of his Dominions.
CORINSILVIUS Shepherds
AMIENSJAQUES Lords attending upon the DUKE in his Banishment
WILLIAM, a Country Fellow, in love
METEOR, a rock from outer space

Pat's hands trembled as he read the cast of characters. Who were these people? He had only written about Frank and Joe and certainly didn't make Joe a brother to a duke!

He decided to read the last act since he knew that as the anchor of the play goes so goes the entire play:

.c. Act V
.c. Scene II. [The forest.]
[Enter JOE and FRANK.]
JOE; Can I tell you a story, Frank?
FRANK; By all means.
JOE; I was walking by a tall tree the other day and I thought I had heard a voice coming from . . .
FRANK; God save you, brother.
JOE; And you, fair sister.
[Exit. JOE] O my dear Frank, how it grieves me to see thee not listen to my tale!
[Enter JOE.]
FRANK; Why, am I not playing the part of an interested listener?
JOE; I thought thy attention had been wounded with the claws of a lion.
FRANK; Wounded it is.
JOE; Do you want me to tell you more?
FRANK; Ay, and greater wonders than that.
JOE; Nay, 'tis true. There was never anything so sudden, but the fight of two rams and Caesar's thrasonical drag . . . of wrath of love . . . clubs cannot part them.
FRANK; I shall be married tomorrow.
JOE; What? You haven't heard one single word.
FRANK; I can no longer play the part of the interested listener.
JOE; I will weary you then no longer with idle talking. Know of me then, for now I . . .
FRANK; Speak'st thou in sober meanings?

JOE; By my life, I do!
[Enter METEOR THROUGH STAGE DOOR]
FRANK; Look, a meteor.

Pat dropped the play. He couldn't believe it! Not only was this blatant Shakespearean plagiarism, but it was also a very poorly written scene!

He eagerly phoned the Jim Bob Playwright Company for a 100% refund.

"Hello, Jim Bob," a voice said.

"Hello this is Pat Jones," Pat said. "I just received my play!"

"Did you say, Pat Jones?" jim Bob said. "The Pat who just had an offer for a Broadway production of his play 'The Meteor'?"

Pat stopped.

"Did you say Broadway?"

"It will be staged in the Alley Theater. Ever hear of it?" Big Jim said.

"The Alley Theater? Who hasn't!?" Pat said, but it was obvious he had not.

"We want to start rehearsals ASAP. You will need to come up with fifty thousand dollars."

"Okay," Pat said. He took out another fifty thousand from his IRA account and mailed it to the Playwright company. They sent him detailed instructions on when and where the rehearsals would be, and Pat quickly got in his car and drove into New York City, checking into the finest hotel that money could put you in.

The following day, Pat drove to the address. It was not on Broadway. It was off-Broadway. In fact, it was in an alley full of garbage cans. Pat couldn't believe it. He had been duped for sure!

But, right at that very moment, while he was chiding himself over and over and over, a meteor hurled itself through the atmosphere and landed right smack on top of Pat's head.

The End

FUND DAY

Every week, without fail, the fund committee would meet to review all funds in their various accounts. The fund managers were present. It was a momentous occasion. There was a rumor already that the company had made a substantial profit.

"Let's start by listing all funds. The small caps, the large caps, the kitty caps . . . " the president paused. "The kitty caps?"

Frank Jones, new fund manager, and all round nice guy, sat staring into space.

"Frank? I believe this is your fund," the president said.

Frank sat still for a little while and finally acknowledged the president.

"The Kitty Kat Fund is a fund made up of all companies that make things for cats."

There was a slight pause.

"How much money has been invested by *cat-lovers* into your fund?"

"Five billion dollars."

"Five billion dollars? That's an impressive amount. How much profit has it made?"

"One hundred two dollars and fifteen cents."

"One hundred two dollars and fifteen cents profit? On five billion dollars?"

"The value of the fund is a hundred two dollars and fifteen cents. I don't know how much profit it's made."

Frank stopped talking and stared off into space.

From the second floor window, the president could hear noises. He looked out and saw many angry people—some with guns.

"Frank! What have you done?"

Frank didn't say a word but stared and stared and stared.

"Frank? Frank?"

There was no response.

"Where's the fund's dossier?"

Frank didn't have anything in front of him. The president motioned the secretary to run and get the dossier from Frank's office. She ran out and immediately came back with a folder that had a little cardboard cat tail hanging off its lower edge. The top edge had cardboard cat ears. The president opened the folder and began to read the list of companies that made up the fund.

"Kitty Kat Meow." The rest of the page was blank. "The following fine products are made by Kitty Kat Meow under the wise, benevolent guidance of founder and CEO Frank Jones: Great Smelling Kitty Kat Meow Litter, Kitty Kat Meow Chow for Growing Kitty Kats, Kitty Kat Meow Dog and Cat Collars, Kitty Kat Meow Moth Balls?"

The president dropped the dossier.

Frank sat very still. His lips were pursed, and he was blowing air through them every so often. The president walked over to where he was sitting and got down to his level.

"Frank?"

Frank continued to stare into space.

"Moth balls, Frank?"

Frank let some more air out of his pursed lips. He didn't care what was happening in the world of high finance. He was a kitty kat.

"Meow."

The End

JUMPING JIM

Jim was an excellent piano player and a great composer. But, he had two bad things going for him. He didn't have a piano, and he was flat broke.

Call it luck, coincidence, or total fatalism, but Jim spoke with his next door neighbor for the first time since he had moved in five years ago. The man, who was middle-aged, became very excited when Jim told him about his life goal. The man promptly took Jim out and bought him the keyboard he wanted.

"And, whatever it takes to make your first recording, I'll pay for that, too," Frank, Jim's neighbor, said.

Jim was overwhelmed with gratitude. He quickly went to work on his songs. Soon, with the help of Frank's money, he made his first recording. The response was overwhelming. Jim was an overnight sensation.

At first, Frank was very adamant about not being paid anything. He had done only what he felt was the right thing to do for such a young, ambitious composer. Maybe this was all he needed to get to heaven?

However, at the insistence of Jim, he finally broke down and accepted the job as Jim's manager. Jim was totally grateful and knew that if it were not for the kindness of this gentleman he would have never made it to the top. Why wouldn't Frank be a great manager, he thought, he's already put me on the top.

The first booking Frank made was in Smallcreek, Arizona, near the Mexican border. It was a small insignificant town with a population of twenty-five, twenty-six, if you count the ninety-six year old patriarch Gonzales who had been on his deathbed since he was seventy. Most of the people lived on welfare; two of them worked at the one gas station in town. If there were a market for tumbleweeds and dust storms, Smallcreek would have been a thriving metropolis and its inhabitant's millionaires. Jim, or Jumping Jim as he was now called, was aghast.

"Why a God forsaken place like Smallcreek, Frank?" Jim asked in total disbelief. "No one will be at my first concert and I'll be the laughingstock of the music industry."

Frank just laughed and gave Jim a knowing look.

"Trust me. It was where my late wife, Edith, and I had our honeymoon. And God hasn't forsaken it. Believe me, you'll be a hit."

Jim couldn't believe it. He had to let Frank go, and he knew it. He now began to understand that the only reason that Frank gave him such a great start was not out of kindness, but out of irrationality. Frank was insane! And now, if he didn't fire him, he would be ruined in less than a week.

"Uh . . . Frank," Jim said after a slight hesitation, "I really believe that Smallcreek is the wrong town for my concert, or any concert for that matter."

"Trust me," Frank said with a big, goofy grin.

"I'm sorry," Jim said. "I made a mistake. You really didn't want to be manager, and I forced you into it. Sorry."

"I just spent a half million on advertising," Frank said ignoring Jim's remarks.

Half a million dollars! Jim was really beginning to regret letting Frank write checks on his bank account. Oh well, Jim thought with a shrug, the money's been spent, he might as well go through with it. However, he was going to grow a mustache and beard and do the concert under a different name. They could announce that Jumping Jim got sick or something and bring on this "new" guy. Knowing that town, they wouldn't be able to tell the difference between a musician and a squealing pig.

"Okay Frank, I'll do this one concert, but you're going to have to retire as my manager right now, for your own good," Jim replied.

Frank nodded and tweaked Jim's nose; something Jim absolutely abhorred. He even did it to him during an important television interview. Jim felt like punching Frank's grinning mug.

When Jim walked outside a brick happened to fall off the top floor and bang him on the head.

"Ouch," he said and then he went bling.

BLING!

"Why . . . Smallcreek, Arizona," he said with growing excitement, "why didn't I think of that? What a fantastic idea!"

When Frank walked out, Jim took his hand and shook it vigorously.

"Thank you, Frank, for being such a good manager! I really don't want you to ever quit," Jim said. "Your idea is excellent. Ouch . . . my head. You are sensational. Spend all the money you want."

"What about giving the entire concert free of charge?" Frank asked.

Jim blinked his eyes several times. He couldn't believe Frank had said that. Why that was the very thought that had just crossed his mind.

"Brilliant!" he said rubbing his head. "Frank, you think of everything."

"Including free transportation to anyone who wants to come," Frank said.

"You said it, babe," Jim said. "Now, let's get this show on the road, darling."

"Can I have a million dollars for myself?" Frank asked.

"You have a contract, I'll sign it," Jim said clapping his hands and doing a little jump. "I'm Jumping Jim. See how high I can jump?"

The word was out! Jumping Jim was doing his first concert, free of charge and with free transportation to anyone who wanted to come. Everyone was talking about it, and the news made the front page of every city and town from Smallcreek to Bigrock. Smallcreek seemed to grow overnight. Frank bought the town and was elected the mayor by an overwhelming majority of twenty-five votes. The patriarch, Gonzales, ran against him but died the night before the election.

The first thing Frank did was to contract out to build a huge one hundred thousand-seat stadium, the likes of which would have never been seen in the whole state. The whole town was employed. Frank was interviewed on every major talk show and made the cover of every financial journal. People seemed to think that he was a financial whiz.

Jumping Jim was not content. He wanted more than ever to have the concert in the desert among the stars, and not in a stadium which would take ten years to construct. He would be forgotten by then. Also, he wasn't content with the musical style he had worked on all his life. He wanted more of an oriental, Arabic style. He even wanted to learn to play the sitar and forget all about the keyboards. In fact, with all the people coming, he would force them to listen by not having an Amp system. There he would be, in the midst of thousands, playing his sitar in the desert among the stars, but he wouldn't tell Frank until the night of the concert, which was ten years away.

Frank was looking at a movie contract when Jim jumped over to him.

"Hey man, what's up?" Frank asked.

"I have decided on a bunny costume," Jim said.

"Say, Jim," Frank said, "someone has offered me a contract to do a movie."

"Am I in it?" Jim asked.

"No," Frank said. "It's an epic and will probably take about three years of my time. So let's just meet back here in ten years when the stadium is finished."

"Sure thing, Frank!" Jim said. "Er, I'll just hop over to the store and get me some carrots. Yesiree Bob."

Ten years passed. Jim's brief career as a rock star plummeted like an avalanche while Frank became a famous movie star. The epic was a huge success and dropped Frank right in the midst of the social elite.

Frank hadn't seen or heard from Jim since the time he hopped off to the store for carrots ten years ago. In fact, Frank had nearly forgotten about their promised meeting at the stadium, which was due for its grand opening in a few days.

Jim woke up to the smell of garbage next to his nose and a dog licking his face. The headache that he had been suffering from for the past ten years was gone! He wondered where he was and then was aghast to look down and see himself attired in some sort of an Easter Bunny suit. It must have been some party last night he thought as he stumbled out of the alley. He had to find Frank and to talk to him about the Smallcreek concert. It couldn't happen! He was a famous rock star and too famous to play in a rinky-dink town like Smallcreek.

But, then Jim stepped on a banana peel and slipped. He hit his head.

"Cheeseburger," Jim said looking up at the dog. "Take me to your leader."

A few days later, Frank arrived with great pomp and circumstance to the opening of the Jumping Jim Memorial Stadium. It was to be dedicated to Jim since no one had heard of him in years.

A huge crowd of celebrities flew in for such a posh ceremony. Several heads of state e-mailed their congratulations for a job well done, and, in the midst of all the excitement, Jim happened to show up with a broken sitar and a torn bunny costume. The problem was, he was in the far back of the great crowd that had assembled while Frank was up front cutting the ribbon to the stadium and receiving accolades upon accolades.

For those unfortunately in the back, Jim began to play his sitar and sing in a whine, every once in a while giving a little jump.

"Hey buddy, shut up the music," One burly man said. "We are trying to listen to the speech."

"I've never been so insulted in all my life," Jim said throwing the sitar to the ground. Everyone in the back applauded.

Jim thought they were applauding his great performance.

"I'm a star," he whispered to himself.

"And now, Ladies and Gentlemen, I will do my famous impersonation of a rabbit eating a sitar," Jim said.

Everyone in the back turned to listen to the speech.

"Ladies and Gentlemen and bald-headed ladies…" the crowd laughed. "We gather here today to pay tribute to a great friend and a great musician, Jumping Jim."

Jim stopped chewing on his sitar and stood up.

"Jim was to do his first concert today, a free concert with free transportation, but he mysteriously disappeared ten years ago. I wish I knew where he was. His very first and only album went platinum the day it hit the record stores. He was wonderful and had so much potential. I really miss him." Frank began to cry. "Jim, if you're watching this ceremony, if you can hear me, I LOVE YOU, BROTHER!"

Yes, it was true! Jim and Frank were actually brothers who had been separated at a very young age when their parents had gotten divorced. Jim was only an infant then, but Frank had been old enough to remember Jim. In fact, that was what led Frank to move into Jim's neighborhood and help him start his music career. He didn't tell Jim or anyone because the fact that Jim was raised in an orphanage and all alone in the world seemed to elicit a lot of sympathy from the fans and boost his popularity.

Jim fell to the ground in a dead faint. Someone screamed for a doctor. Frank noticed the commotion in the back and sent one of his aides to check it out.

The End

DISPOSABLE ART

It was an age of commercialism. It was also an age of recycling. Advertising was rampant, but so was the fact that anything anyone bought would be recyclable. Recycling had gone the extra mile—so to say—so that all interest groups would be satisfied. Not only was the standard fare recyclable—bottles, newspapers, and old women—but the roads, buildings, cars, trains, planes, and anything else anyone owned. In fact, recycling had become so refined that after a few years everything reverted to dust so that nature was totally unspoiled.

Of course, this was great for the economy. Construction was at an all time high. With everything disintegrating left and right, construction had to constantly make repairs, rebuild the highways, and reconstruct the bridges that so daintily fell out of the sky as colorful dust into the rivers below. The time for anything to revert to nature was so well known, that everything had a sticker showing the date of expiration so that young couples could move to a larger home, cars wouldn't drive over "daintily falling out of the sky" bridges and companies could expand without worrying about the debris they left behind. It was a beautiful time in the world. Clean air, clean water in abundance, and everything turning into dust left and right at the drop of a bucket.

Unfortunately, it wasn't really a good time for artists. Anything they drew or painted on, or anything they sculptured for that matter, would also turn to dust after so many years. There weren't many claims to fame to something that no one would see that sat in some disposable studio for years before being discovered. For all that would be discovered would be a big pile of dust, and that probably would not even be seen since the wind surely would have blown it away.

So artists had to adjust themselves to the fact that their sole purpose in life was to create only for the now and then. The name everyone gave to this form of genre was "Disposable Art." There was a dilemma, however. For how was an artist to get his artwork seen and ever be remembered as a great artist?

The solution was quickly realized. The best way to have one's artwork seen was to advertise and to put the art on giant billboards and signs all over the country. The people would be able to stop and admire the artwork and be able to distinguish who was the best artist and who was indeed the worst. Without this type of display, the artist might as well become a seller of disposable brushes for his art would never be seen and would quickly turn to dust.

Therefore, it happened. The best artists became society's greatest commercial artists. When a corporation wanted to sell a car, a famous artist was quickly commissioned and soon an oil painting in shocking photo-realism would soon embrace a prominent spot in the city where not only would people stop and ravenously desire the car, but would also bring picnic lunches and camp out at the local park and sit and admire the great art, having deep discussions on the philosophical relevance of the style of painting and whether or not the car was actually a painting or real and stuff like that.

Of course, with so much competition to get work recognized before it turned to dust, the great disposable society did not have much free time to spare for mediocre artists. Fred, who loved to paint little rabbits and cows and other animals in the fields and forests, was not spared by the competition. No one liked his art. Fred suggested, to all whom would listen, that his broad strokes and bold lines of animals whose legs seemed to come to a sharp point and men who stood by them with spears were actually a form of modern expressionism. Of course, most people wouldn't listen. They would either hold their ears or simply give Fred a pat on the back and encourage him to find professional help.

Fred was quite despondent to say the least. After a series of rejections, and seeing no hope for the media ever to hype his artwork, Fred soon began to lose interest in art and in life in general. And, right when he began to have thoughts of finding a soon to be expiring bridge to stand on, the telephone rang and Farmer McGarver called on Fred to help him advertise his farm produce.

"Really? You mean it?" Fred asked.

"How soon can you get some ads out?" Farmer McGarver asked.

"As soon as I can find a disposable billboard," Fred said. When Fred hung up the phone, he was very happy. He was going to paint a masterpiece!

Unfortunately, Fred was unable to find any disposable billboard or any disposable paint for that matter. All of it had been sold, and the existing stock had already reverted to its natural state. It would be months before new disposable billboard or paint would be fabricated. Fred was in despair and Farmer McGarver's livestock was soon dying off before being sold.

After a series of life threatening phone calls from Farmer McGarver, Fred finally said his ad would be ready in the morning. Fred told him that he had found some medium to advertise his livestock and that it was something that wasn't on disposable billboard or with disposable paint, but it would still be considered recyclable. Farmer McGarver didn't care as long as his ad was up the next day.

And now, my dear readers, this is where this story begins to turn for the worse. The next morning, when Farmer McGarver came to see his ad, Fred didn't show him a sign that could be displayed in some prominent site in the city, but a stone wall where he had painted Farmer McGarver's animals and had attached the ad copy with big disposable letters. Farmer McGarver was fit to be tied! Fred explained to Farmer McGarver that the stone wall would eventually turn to dust although it would take considerably longer than a few hundred years, but this was not why Farmer McGarver was mad. Fred had not only painted his animals on a stone wall, but he had painted them inside a cave where no one in their right mind would venture and surely no one would ever see the advertisement.

So Fred was a failure and soon disintegrated into obscurity.

Of course, the media makes or breaks a person. After many years, when the disposable society had vanished without a trace and their dust was recycled to make other useful products for mankind, when their language began to take on its own style and some people in that part of the world began the day by saying "Bonjour" to one another, a small boy tossed a ball into a hole in the ground. And when he ventured into the hole to look for the ball, he discovered strange paintings of animals and men with spears.

And that, my dear readers, was how, after thousands of years, Fred, whom society had shunned during his lifetime, was finally recognized as an artist.

The End

WELCOME TO THE FAMILY

Sophia brushed her long blonde hair out of her eyes. Her blue eyes looked up ever so gently at her fiancé, Guido. His stout nose and curly black hair went perfectly with the rest of his face. He even had black eyes. And a pair of hands. And some legs. And feet.

Sophia laughed gently at Guido who had just made a little funny. She laughed at everything Guido said to her. She was the perfect date.

"Ha-ha, that is so rich!" Sophia said. "How can you be so handsome and so funny at the same time?"

Guido took this as a compliment and raised his eyebrows up and down. He reached over and grabbed Sophia's hand. He desperately needed her. He couldn't wait another minute. They had to be wed. Soon!

"Say you will come to my house tomorrow and meet my parents," Guido said.

Sophia laughed.

"No, really. This time I mean it," Guido said. "I want you to meet them. I know they will love you as much as I do. Please say you will meet them."

Sophia laughed again and slapped her knees. Tears started coming out of her eyes.

"You're such a scream!"

Guido sat back in his chair and looked out over the ocean. A nice summer breeze was blowing in on a fine evening. The sun had just gone down for the night. The stars were beginning to pop out of their daytime hiding place.

Guido clasped his hands and looked upward.

"Oh, please God," he prayed silently, "let this be the one."

When Guido looked back at Sophia, she was looking at him with a silly smirk on her face. Her lips were tightly shut, but she couldn't keep the laughter from coming out. She spit out a little laugh, then another, and finally she just guffawed out loud.

"Ha, ha, ha. How can you be so funny? Ha, ha, ha."

"Sophia, please."

Sophia suddenly took a hold of the tablecloth and fell on the ground dragging the dishes with it. She rolled over holding her stomach.

"Ha, ha, ha!"

Guido grabbed the end of the tablecloth and pulled as hard as he could.

Sophia grabbed the other end and was yanked to her feet.

"So! My playful little Guido," Sophia giggled, "you want to play tug of war, too?"

Guido was amazed at Sophia's strength. Every time he gained an inch, Sophia would pull and he would be dragged at least a foot. Beads of sweat appeared on his forehead.

"Sophia, please let go of the tablecloth so I can reset the table for dinner tonight!" Guido shouted.

Sophia burst out laughing which temporarily loosened her death grip on the edge of the tablecloth. Guido triumphantly gave the tablecloth a final tug that sent Sophia sprawling face down onto the floor. Guido was horrified.

"Sophia, my darling, are you alright?" Guido asked, full of concern.

Sophia lay still, still as death.

"Sophia!" Guido screamed. "Answer me. Oh no! Answer me!"

Guido began to cry when Sophia suddenly let out a loud laugh.

"Fooled you, fooled you," she cried as she pointed a finger at him. "You are so funny! Oh, my stomach hurts."

With that, she clutched her sides, rolling around the floor with big tears of laughter rolling down her cheeks.

"Foolish woman!" Guido said and turned and walked away.

"Guido! Wait. What time do you want me to meet your parents?"

Guido stopped. He didn't know what it was that possessed him so to love this girl, but she could mock him and laugh at him, and his heart would still pound out her name with every beat.

"Seven," he said.

"Don't be late, you naughty man!" Sophia said and began to laugh again.

Guido walked away. Hopefully, Sophia wouldn't laugh so much around his parents, Irwin and Winkle Smith.

"You naughty man! Ha, ha, ha!" Sophia screamed after him. "You naughty, naughty man!"

The next evening, Guido arrived at Sophia's house dressed in a white tuxedo and driving a red luxury sports car. He opened the car door and hopped out.

When he walked up to the beach front condo, Sophia suddenly walked out of the front door with a beautiful long white silken dress, elegant white gloves, and her hair pulled back with a diamond comb. Her makeup was professional. Her jeweled case white purse accented the diamonds around her neck and dangling from her ears.

"Sophia. What a breath of fresh air," Guido said.

"Don't look at me. I am horrible!" Sophia suddenly said and burst out crying.

"Sophia, you look beautiful," Guido said and took hold of her arm.

Sophia couldn't stop crying.

"It's no use. I'm so ugly."

Guido didn't know what to say and just steered her towards his car. Sophia took one look at the splendid car and screamed.

"I'm not worthy to sit in this beautiful car!"

"Sophia," Guido pleaded, "I don't know what has gotten into you! You're beautiful. You're the most beautiful woman that I have ever known! This is the only car worthy of your loveliness!"

"Nooo," Sophia wailed, "I won't ride in it, I won't, I tell you, I won't!"

With that, Sophia collapsed in a sobbing heap in front of her condo. Guido had no choice but to hail a taxi. A dirty cab stopped in front of them. The driver was dressed in an undershirt with parts of his last meal splattered over the front. A baseball cap sat on top of his head, and a cigarette dangled from his lips.

"You folks going to the opera or something?" he muttered.

Guido was starting to feel that his evening was beginning to fall apart and it hadn't even started! He hesitated to get into that filthy cab with his white tuxedo but had no choice when the driver began to honk his horn. Sophia shielded her face as she got in the cab, hoping that the driver wouldn't notice her ugliness.

"Opera House?" the driver asked.

Guido began to give the driver his parents' address when Sophia interrupted.

"Yes, Opera," Sophia answered, "and quickly. We're running late."

Guido's jaw dropped, and he attempted to say something but the words seemed to be stuck in his throat. All he could manage was a little sputter.

The driver turned on the meter and started off towards the Opera House.

After a few minutes, Guido regained his composure and endeavored to correct this disastrous turn of events. He took a quick look at Sophia. She was sleeping. Guido quickly slipped a twenty to the driver.

"I would like you to take us to 254 Maple Street instead of . . . "

The driver saw the twenty and immediately stepped on the gas.

"We'll be at the Opera House in ten minutes! Yessiree!" he said with a chuckle.

"Irwin, are they here yet?" Winkle asked her husband. He looked out their front window into the evening air.

"I don't see any car yet. Wait. Maybe that's them coming down the road."

"Why don't you go out and greet them," Winkle said.

Irwin quickly walked out of the house and to the curb where the afternoon rain had gently accumulated. Irwin stood there with his arm up as though to wave a greeting to some young woman, but, instead of greeting a woman, Irwin greeted a big splash of water that was mercilessly thrown on him by a passing dirty cab. Winkle let out a scream from inside the house when she saw what had happened. She immediately ran outside, and, when she did, she tripped over the lawn sprinkler and fell face down into the curb where an equal amount of water, which had splashed on her husband, cushioned her fall.

"Where am I?" Sophia suddenly said waking up and looking about her.

Guido looked at her in disgust.

"I hope you enjoyed your little nap. The opera is almost over."

"Opera?" Sophia said and looked around her. She was indeed in the Opera House, in one of the nicest seats in the house, and had a big blanket tucked around her with a little pillow under her head.

"Guido? How did we get here?" she asked.

"You wanted to come here," Guido said.

"No," Sophia said.

"You told the taxi driver to take us to the opera," Guido said.

"Silly me!" Sophia said and began to laugh. "What on earth could I have been thinking?"

"If we hurry now we may be able to salvage this evening," Guido said.

Sophia was quickly on her feet.

"Let's go, my love," Sophia said.

"Yeah, yeah," Guido said.

"What's wrong? Guido, are you mad at me?" Sophia asked.

"I don't want to discuss this any further."

"Guido. No. Don't be angry. I will not do this again."

Guido walked away without speaking another word. Suddenly,

Sophia began to cry again. Guido stopped. Her crying melted away his anger. How could he ever hate such a woman?

"Alright. I'm sorry," Guido said.

"Say you will never be angry with me again," Sophia said and clasped his arm with her dainty hands.

"Never," Guido said and smiled at her. She was his precious prize.

Once outside, Guido hailed a taxi and Sophia hopped in smiling at her fiancé. Guido got in after her and told the taxi driver to go to his parent's house. When he looked back at Sophia, he was surprised to see her shielding her face with the Opera Program.

"No! Don't look at me! I am so ugly!" Sophia cried.

Guido didn't know what to do. He hoped that she would be okay by the time they got to his parent's house, but, to his further embarrassment, Sophia started to put a lot of makeup on her already beautifully made up face.

"Sophia. You look beautiful already. You don't need any more makeup."

Sophia didn't listen. She started to cake on foundation all over her face. In the glow of the passing streetlights, Guido could make out the words "Halloween" and "Clown" on the makeup case.

"Uh . . . Sophia? What kind of makeup are you using?"

Sophia finished blacking out one of her front teeth and turned around to face Guido's horrified face.

"Be a clown, be a clown, everyone loves a clown . . . " Sophia sang with her arms outstretched. The taxi driver joined in heartily.

"How about this one?" the driver asked as he broke into a very poor rendition of "Send in the Clowns."

"Stop the cab!" Sophia screamed. The driver pulled over, and Sophia dashed out of the taxi. In the glow of a street lamp, Sophia began a mime show. The driver clapped gleefully, got out, and showed off his dance steps. A passerby threw them a quarter. Both of them dived for it as Guido watched, stupefied, from the cab. Sophia and the taxi driver hit their heads together as the quarter rolled into a gutter.

"Ouch! My head!" Sophia muttered as she rubbed her head. "Where am I?"

"Sophia! Are you okay?" Guido said. Sophia looked up at him in a daze.

"Yes," she said and got back into the cab.

For the rest of the trip there was nothing but silence. When they finally arrived at 254 Maple Street, Sophia didn't say a word but looked out the window.

"Er, Sophia," Guido said, "don't you think you should have let the taxi driver back into his cab instead of getting in and driving away?"

"Oh, Guido. What is wrong with me?" Sophia suddenly said and began to cry again. "I don't know what has happened to me."

Winkle and Irwin saw the cab pull up and quickly turned out the lights. Winkle had baked a huge triple decker white frosted cake.

"I am so excited!" Winkle said.

"Calm down, Mother," Irwin said. "It's just your only son and future daughter-in-law."

Winkle did a little wiggle dance and deftly balanced the cake in her hands.

She stood beside the front door.

"Don't tell them I am here," she said to Irwin. "I want to jump out and yell 'SURPRISE' when they walk through the door."

Irwin winked knowingly at his wife. He adjusted his bow tie. He couldn't wait to meet his son and his future wife.

"My face!" Sophia screamed suddenly seeing herself in the rear-view mirror. "What has happened to my face?"

Sophia got out of the cab and started to run to the front door. "Must make it to the bathroom before his parents see me."

"Sophia!" Guido yelled after her.

Sophia didn't listen and opened Irwin and Winkle's front door with a bang.

"Must find a bathroom!" she screamed and ran into the house crying and holding her hands over her face.

The front door started to close. Guido flung the door open with another bang!

"Sophia!" Guido yelled.

"Guido, no!" Irwin yelled.

The front door slowly swung shut to reveal Winkle standing there with her lovely triple-decker, white-frosted cake smashed into her face. She was wearing the top layer like a little pillbox hat. A gurgling noise appeared to be coming from her throat.

"Momma!" Guido shouted.

"M-m-my cake . . ." Winkle said slowly, ". . . m-m-my beautiful cake!"

Guido tried to find some humor in this otherwise very awkward situation.

"I'm sorry, Momma," Guido said.

Winkle let out a little sob and ran upstairs, leaving the top layer in Guido's hands. Guido turned to his father.

"Hi, Papa," said Guido. "What's up?"

The sight of his one and only son's face made Irwin quickly forget the events of the past few moments. He gave his son a big bear hug and felt something squishy between them. They both looked down and saw that they each had half of the cake on their chests. They burst out laughing.

A few minutes passed and suddenly Winkle made an appearance at the head of the stairs.

"Look who I found!" she said.

Guido looked up and noticed that both Sophia and his mother had on matching bathrobes and towels around their heads.

"I'll be right back," he said as he dashed upstairs.

"Why, Irwin," Winkle exclaimed, "isn't that my cake that you are wearing on your chest?"

"I'll be right back," Irwin said as he dashed upstairs.

A few minutes later, they both appeared with big turbans on their heads.

"Hello, darlings."

"Why, Irwin and Guido," Winkle said, "aren't those our beach towels?"

Sophia began to laugh and snort.

"I have something for you," Winkle said to Sophia and ran off. Soon, she came back holding a big box. "It's my wedding gown. I believe you will be able to wear it."

"Oh, thank you mother," Sophia said.

Winkle started to cry when she heard the word "mother."

"Hey, what is that funny smell coming from the kitchen?" Guido said.

"My roasted chestnut pie!" Winkle screamed.

Smoke bellowed out of the kitchen, and soon fire began to engulf the dry wood.

"Quick. Get something to put out the fire!" Sophia screamed and grabbed Winkle's box and threw it into the kitchen.

"Everybody out of the house!" Guido screamed and guided his shocked mother and father out onto the lawn. Sophia ran out and fell on the lawn gasping.

"Oh, what a night this is," she said.

"You . . . you threw my wedding dress into the fire," Winkle cried.

"My house. My house for 40 years. Going up in smoke!" Irwin said.

"My future wife," Guido said getting down on the grass and holding Sophia's hands.

"Guido," Sophia said, "my love for you will never wane."

Suddenly, a very out of breath taxi driver came running up the block.

"Hey lady, you took my cab!" he said. "I'm calling the police!"

Winkle and Irwin stood still, in a state of shock, while Guido looked at Sophia.

"You are under arrest," Guido said and held up his police badge.

The End

JO LENA

If you ever ask, you can be shown the pecan trees on the ranch. Sit on a nice wooden porch, gaze over a nicely manicured lawn, a chain-link fence, and a grassy glen that slightly slopes to the pecan orchard. You can see a little creek that runs across the property and, sometimes, a cow or two that will wander across the creek, walk through the orchard and up to the grassy glen where they will eat all the grass. The cows won't touch the pecan trees. The giraffes won't either.

Jo Lena can tell you that lightning bolts can hit a pecan tree and rot out its insides so it eventually falls to the ground with a loud bang. The cows don't mind, but the giraffes get mighty upset.

One day, some weeks ago, Jo Lena got a call from one of the cow owners. He was not in a good mood. An elephant had stepped on one of his cows.

"Now, Jo Lena, I know you went crazy and put all these wild animals all over your property, but I put my cows on your property so your property taxes won't be so high and you can have some free fertilizer from time to time, but I didn't put my cows on your property so they can be stepped on by elephants."

"If the cow didn't get in the elephant's way, it wouldn't have been squushed," Jo Lena said and proceeded to stare.

"Jo Lena, we're talking about a Texas ranch here. There are no elephants on a Texas ranch."

"They are on mine."

"I have a right mind to move my herd across the road to the Richardson's ranch. They don't have any elephants on their ranch. You'd lose your tax status. What do you think about that?"

"The elephants would track them down and squish them anyway," Jo Lena said. "That cow must've insulted the herd or something. That's why the elephant stepped on it. The elephant herd doesn't like being insulted."

"That's foolish talk."

"I think you better leave before my monkeys let the air out of your truck."

The cow owner turned around and saw a chimp with a screwdriver. On the other side of the truck was Jo Lena's husband.

"What's this?"

"You better go now before an elephant falls out of the sky and squishes you just like that cow."

"You have gone totally insane, Jo Lena! You haven't heard the last of this!" The cow owner got into his truck. "That rhino has driven you mad!"

Jo Lena stood still, stared, and watched him leave. After he crossed the creek, she told the monkeys to get back to work.

Poor Jo Lena. Many months before this incident, she had been such an example of social perfection—Leander's shining star. Her country home and grounds had been written up in the state's good living magazines. She was meticulous about being a good hostess, a good homemaker, and a good housekeeper. Nothing was left to be a rebuke or a sight for sore eyes. Everything was in place. There was a time and place for everything, and the people of Leander looked to Jo Lena for the time and place.

Jo Lena had always been a hearty worker at her church. The church was small—about 150 people. One day, the church got together and decided to give Jo Lena a token of their appreciation. So, while she was sleeping, they sneaked onto her property and placed a life-size rhino statue on her front lawn—fresh from Leander's Animal Sculpture Farm.

Jo Lena got up out of bed and said, "It's a beautiful day, Lord," and then proceeded to scream. "There's a rhino on my front lawn!"

She ran outside and looked this way and that.

"Praise the Lord there is no one around," she said and ran into the house.

"Quick, get up," she said to her husband.

"What?" Her husband stirred.

"We got to get that rhino off our property. We'll be the laughingstock."

"Rhino?"

Jo Lena hit her husband with a pillow.

"There is no time to explain. Get up and get the truck!"

Jo Lena's sister, May Lana, had moved from Illinois to retire on the ranch. She and her husband had built a beautiful home with a nice vegetable garden in the front. May always rose later than Jo Lena. On this particular day, she arose and went into the kitchen to get some coffee. When she picked up the pot, she immediately dropped it on the floor. She quickly put her face to the kitchen window. There, in her vegetable garden, crushing the okra plants, was a rhino statue. She saw Jo Lena's truck hurriedly leaving her property.

"No!"

After a few minutes, knowing her sister had probably arrived home, May Lana called Jo Lena.

"Jo Lena, did you put a rhino in my garden?"

"Er . . . er . . . er," Jo Lena stuttered.

"You get that hideous thing out of my garden, and right now!"

"I thought you might want it."

"No."

"Well, the church gave it to us and it looks horrible in our front yard. I can't give it back. Please keep it in your vegetable garden."

"Jo Lena, you come over here this instance."

"What am I going to do with it?"

"That's your problem. Give it to June."

Jo Lena paused for a second. Why that was an idea. June was an old cousin of Jo Lena's who had a one-room house built up in the hills. She didn't have anything in her yard but a few sunflowers and some old tires.

"And now," Jo Lena thought, "a beautiful rhino statue."

It wasn't more than an hour later, that a very anxious June called Jo Lena's house.

"There's a rhino on my lawn. He's going to charge the house any second." June was fit to be tied.

"June, there are no rhinos in Texas. It's a statue," Jo Lena said.

"No, I saw it move. Please, come over and get it. You have a truck."

"No, June, it's a statue. We put it there this morning. Surprise."

"Please. It's scaring me."

Jo Lena and her husband drove over and picked up the rhino. June peered out behind the curtains but never came out. She wasn't going to come out for another month. There was bound to be another rhino in that neck of the woods. If there was one, then there was another.

"Well, what do we do now?" Jo Lena's husband asked.

"Put it on Carroll property. They will appreciate it."

It wasn't more than a week later that the head of the Carroll family phoned Jo Lena.

"The real estate agent says he can't sell any of our land if there is a rhino on it. We know you put it there. You come and get it."

Jo Lena sighed. That rhino was getting to be a nuisance. Without telling her husband, she drove the truck over to the Carroll's and managed to get the rhino into the truck. When her husband came back from work and was about to drive across the creek, he immediately stopped his car. There was the rhino standing in the creek. On the other side was Jo Lena.

"I thought he might be used as a stepping stone, in case the water gets too high," she said.

"Jo Lena, I don't care how you do it, but I want you to get rid of this thing. Hide it in the woods somewhere where no one will ever see it."

"Okay," Jo Lena said, "I'll get rid of it. Don't worry."

The next day, Jo Lena's husband came home and never saw the rhino. He was curious.

"Jo Lena! Where did you put the rhino?"

Jo Lena didn't say a word. What her husband wouldn't know, wouldn't hurt him.

"There's a rhino in my sanctuary. There's a rhino in my sanctuary," Pastor said over and over. He was rocking back and forth a little—every once in a while giving a little laugh.

When the good people of Leander heard what had happened, there was nothing but gossip. Jo Lena—the shining star—had fallen.

"They meant well," the neighbors said. "She might have well spit in their face."

"She could have put the rhino in the backyard—behind the shed—if she really didn't like it in the front yard."

"Can you believe the insolence?"

"God's going to punish her. He's going to teach her there's more to life than just a nice home and a nice yard."

Jo Lena got into her car to go to her weekly beauty appointment. She tried to avoid looking at the people while she was driving, but she could feel their stares and scowls. She stopped at a stoplight and casually glanced over at the occupant of a pickup truck.

It was the pastor!

He was laughing and waving.

Jo Lena looked straight ahead. What was she going to do? The light refused to change. The pastor was still waving and had rolled down his window. Jo Lena felt compelled to do the same.

"Rhino Day," the pastor said. "Don't forget to bring your friends. Have them come up and get their picture taken with the rhino."

Jo Lena's eyes opened wide.

"Rhino Day?"

"We'll have a genuine pith helmet there and a hunting rifle," the pastor said. "Don't forget. This is going to be a real blessing."

The light changed and Jo Lena quickly took off. She looked back in her rear view mirror and saw the pastor still sitting there with a big, goofy grin on his face and every once in a while doing a little clap.

"What have I done?" she thought.

When she got to the beauty shop, the women immediately stopped their talking and didn't say much. Eileen, who had been there for ages, came and took Jo Lena's hand.

"Don't mind them, I'll do your hair in a private booth."

Jo Lena sat down and Eileen proceeded to fix the grays in Jo Lena's hair.

"I'm out of the regular highlight, but I want to try this product from Britain."

"Whatever," Jo Lena said feeling rather depressed.

Eileen went to work. After a few minutes, Jo Lena could feel the stuff working.

"Boy, that's quick."

Suddenly, Jo Lena's sat straight up in her chair.

"My scalp is on fire!"

Eileen removed the plastic net and quickly washed the solution out of Jo Lena's hair, but it was too late. Jo Lena's hair was standing straight up, burnt and frazzled. Jo Lena looked at herself in the mirror. She looked like a native woman.

"Booga boo!"

"We can put little red ribbons all over your hair until it grows out," Eileen offered.

"No," Jo Lena said and got up. She walked out of the booth, and all the women stopped and stared. Eileen followed her out.

"I'm so sorry."

"No," Jo Lena said. "You aren't sorry. You are against me. You all are against me! All because of that stinking rhino. You think I should have kept it on my property. You think I should have been sooo grateful. Well, let me tell you something . . . let me tell you one thing . . ."

Right then, Jo Lena stopped talking. The solution had gone through her scalp and fried her brain.

"I'll say one thing . . ."

Everyone waited for her to say it.

"One thing," Jo Lena said. "There! I said it."

Jo Lena started to laugh.

"You want me to have a rhino on my property? Well, let me tell you, not only a rhino but a hippopotamus, too!"

With those words, Jo Lena left and drove straight to Leander's Animal Statue Farm. When the owner saw her, he quickly hid behind the desk.

"Now Jo Lena, don't go throw any shoes at me. I just sold them the rhino."

"Henry, get up behind that counter. I have come here today to buy everything in your store."

Henry timidly looked up.

"You . . . you want to buy everything?"

"I want the big fat stone gorilla, the stone elephants, the stone zebras, the stone coyotes . . . I even want that huge hippo with its mouth wide open. Deliver them all to my ranch and as soon as possible."

"Jo Lena . . . er . . . I appreciate your business, but . . ."

"But nothing. I want them all. You know I have the money to pay for them. I may have panned out as Miss Socialite, but my fame is going to be in these stone animals." Jo Lena paused. "Jo Lena's Magnificent Stone Zoo—the World's Greatest Stone Zoo."

Going on ahead a few months, Jo Lena watched the cow owner drive off and across the creek. There were stone animals all over the ranch—along with a few live giraffes and elephants for atmosphere. At first, Jo Lena had charged admission to her zoo, but, after awhile, she noticed the tourists were not as tidy as she had hoped. She also had to keep on washing the stone animals and the tourists were always in the way. Finally, she just kicked all the tourists out and closed the zoo. Now that she had stone animals, she was going to make sure they were well-taken care of.

Jo Lena watched her husband pull up with a load of gravel.

"You can start with the stone lions, then the zebras, and finally the big mouthed hippo. Just dump the gravel near their mouths. They'll eat it."

Jo Lena noticed the chimpanzee driving the truck.

"And don't forget the rhino!"

The End

A SPRING LOVE STORY

"Likewise, I'm sure," Laura said. "You should have been there. Jake was all alone . . . "

"For awhile," Robert said. ". . . and then he stayed with Marilyn all night long."

"Yes, all night long," Laura said.

"Oh . . . " Maureen said. "I see."

With that smug piece of gossip, Laura and Robert got up to leave. Not knowing why she did it, Maureen suddenly grabbed Laura's sleeve and asked her to stay.

"Oh, okay, Maureen," Laura suddenly replied in a timid voice, "Sure, I'll stay with you as long as you want."

"Well, I'm not staying," Robert replied in a huff, "I've got better things to do with my time."

Laura had about as much of Robert as she could stand for one day.

"Then go and may you never have a moment's peace with your time," she screamed.

Robert couldn't believe that this was the woman that he was going to marry and had taken to the ball. He left without even saying good-bye.

Laura collapsed on the settee, sobbing uncontrollably. Maureen felt a sudden wave of compassion for her and put her arm around Laura's quaking shoulders to calm her.

"I have a great idea," she said.

Laura looked up at her face expectantly, waiting for her calming words of assurance.

"Let's put on a Gala Riverside Exclusive Country Club talent show!" she screamed.

Laura was taken aback.

"What . . . what did you say?" she asked.

"I said a talent show, honey," Maureen said. "Now, say goodbye to all your troubles and fill in the blanks on this talent show form."

"But . . . but . . ." Laura said. "I can't sing. I can't dance."

"Yeah, who can," Maureen said, "Now get up, get out of here, and start signing up high society debutantes like yourself."

"Can I sign up Robert, too?" Laura asked.

"Yeah, sure, why not," Maureen answered. "Sign up everybody on the street for that matter."

"Wow, gee, thanks Maureen. You are a real pal," Laura said.

"Anytime," Maureen said.

"Yes, I really mean it," Laura said.

"Yeah, I know, don't mention it," Maureen said.

"And . . . " Laura asked, "can we ask the country club to let in anybody to see the show?"

"Yeah, sure, why not?" Maureen said. "Have it in the civic center down the street."

Jake was looking over some briefs in his golf cart when a flyer flew across the golf course and right into Brandon's hands. What he read he couldn't believe in a million years!

"Jake, you won't believe what Maureen's been up to!" he screamed. "Here, read this!"

He tossed a flyer onto Jake's lap. Jake picked it up, and what he read literally made his eyes pop out of his head.

> First Annual Riverside Country Club Talent Show. Say goodbye to all your troubles.
> Everyone welcome. Come one, come all!

And, to top it off, a small footnote on the bottom of the flyer announced:

None other than the one and only Jake Thompson III will host the night of music, fun, and laughs!

Brandon had to laugh at the expression on Jake's face. He wished he had a camera so he could snap a picture for all eternity, or at least until he got married and had children who would rip it up.

When Jake had recovered from the shock, he hollered red-faced, "I never conceded to host this farce! I'm going over to talk to Maureen right now. Why, she's mad, I tell you, absolutely mad!"

He was so mad the veins started pulsating in his head.

"Now, now, Jake," Brandon said, "you are just a little upset about this talent show. You need to talk to Maureen and have her take your name off the show."

"Talk to her? Talk to her?" Jake screamed. "Yes, I am going to talk to her all right. Oh yes . . . ha, ha . . . I am going to have a real good talk with her."

"Now, Jake," Brandon warned, "don't do anything rash. You know Maureen always has a good reason for everything she does."

"Ha, ha, ha, look at me, I'm Peter Pan!" Jake said, getting out of the golf cart. He ran and did a little somersault. "No invisible wires or nothing!"

"Uh . . ." Brandon said, "why don't we go to the clubhouse and have lunch."

"Lunch?!" Jake screamed, laughed, and clapped his hands. "Never! I've got to practice! I'm going to be on Broadway!"

"Oh, come on Jake. Put a lid on it!" Brandon said. "I am going to lunch. I'm starved!"

The headwaiter met them at the door.

"Just a moment, sirs, where do you think you're going?" he asked snottily.

"Don't you recognize us?" Jake asked incredulously. "We're Mr. Thompson III and Mr. Williams from the law office of Thompson, Williams, and Smith."

"Is that so?" the headwaiter replied suspiciously. "Then, where is Mr. Smith?"

Jake couldn't believe his ears. Robert Smith had been dead for the past five years, a well-known fact. Murdered, in fact, and they never did find the killer.

"Six feet under," Brandon answered crudely. "You know this!"

They suddenly heard someone gasp and start to cry uncontrollably. To their horror, they discovered that it was none other than Maureen herself. Maureen Smith—the daughter of the late Smith and Jake's fiancée. The headwaiter shrugged nonchalantly when Jake glared at him.

"Well, I was just kidding," he said.

The headwaiter walked them over to where Maureen was seated.

"I . . . I don't know what to say," Maureen said.

"Nor do I," Brandon said.

"Ditto," Jake said.

A long ensuing icy silence followed. Meanwhile, the headwaiter needed to take their order as there was a long line waiting for lunch outside due to the hurricane blowing in earlier than expected.

"Would you care to order, now?" The headwaiter said with a heavy emphasis on the word "now."

Jake slipped him a fiver and he promptly left.

"Well," said Jake, "it looks like we are all here and that we have a quorum."

Everyone agreed.

"I say let's go ahead with this infernal talent show idea that Maureen has worked up, and let's just say for good measure that I have graciously consented to host it," Jake said.

Suddenly, tears welled up in Maureen's eyes. Was this the man whom she said that she could never learn to love again? Suddenly, the love she had forgotten swelled up inside of her and she was totally, crazily, madly in love with Jake Thompson III all over again.

Maureen threw her arms around Jake and gave him a big hug. Jake was taken aback by this sudden show of public affection from Maureen but was completely enjoying it. Jake glanced at Brandon smugly and was glad to see that he was sullen. Jake knew that

Brandon's wife was the ultimate ice queen, and if anyone was starved for affection, Brandon was to Ethiopian standards—Famished, malnutrition, dying.

"Mauree-ee-een!" a voice from across the clubhouse rang out. "Dah-ling!"

Brandon looked up shocked. It was his wife, Cynthia, in a full length formal.

"Oh, there you are, you naughty boy," Cynthia said to Brandon and gave him a big sloppy kiss all over his face. "You can't hide from me."

She sat down on his lap and gave him a big hug.

"Oh, Maureen," she said, "why didn't you tell me about this talent show? It has completely revitalized my life. I haven't been on the stage in years. I can see it now. Cynthia B. Williams live on the New York stage after an absentia of thirty years."

"New . . . New York," said Maureen. "Why, no, Cynthia, it is going to be in the Riverside Civic Center."

"Oh, posh," Cynthia said. "It's going to be in New York City and that's final. I have made up the final posters now being distributed around the city."

Maureen was handed one of the posters and what she saw literally made her head spin. There in large print were the words:

> Cynthia B. Williams-Live on stage
> after a thirty-year absentia—and friends.

And to make matters worse, in small letters:

> None other than the fabulous Maureen and her lovely
> dancing horse, Jake Thompson III,
> will host this gala occasion.

"I'm a dancing horse, too?" Jake said.

"The only thing correct about this flyer is that I'm fabulous," Maureen interjected.

"Neigh, neigh," Jake said, and he got up and pranced around the restaurant.

Brandon sat there in total confusion. First, this sudden outburst of affection from his wife, and then, Jake's behavior.

"I hate horses," Brandon interrupted, "and I'm hungry. Let's order."

Cynthia still sat on Brandon's lap, making it extremely difficult for him to see the menu.

"I'll have the Crock . . . er . . . Croque Monsieur and a Perrier," he told the waiter.

Jake yanked the menu from Brandon's hands.

"How about a burger instead?" he said. "I'll treat you all to some really juicy burgers!"

Everyone cheered heartily except Brandon who tried to protest but was muffled by the yards of ruffles on Cynthia's evening gown. He got up suddenly and walked out of the restaurant in a huff. Cynthia followed him, wailing. She was wailing for a burger, medium soda and fries, the special that she remembered was running that day for only $1.50. With the amount of money she would save by eating at Burger Palace instead, let's say, Burger Castle, she would be able to buy another poster board for the talent show.

"Hurry up!" Brandon hissed thinking her infernal screaming was for him.

"Burger, soda, and some fries, give me some now before I's dies," Cynthia sang out and pirouetted on one foot with her evening gown flowing outward and right in Brandon's face.

Brandon, now red-hot mad, suddenly screamed out:

"What's gotten into you, Cynthia? You've never acted like this before!"

Cynthia stopped dancing and looked at Brandon like a calf looking at a new gate.

"Why, what's gotten into you, Brandon? You've never acted like this before, either," she said. "I know what your problem is.

You're jealous of Jake because he was selected to be the Master of Ceremonies in this once-in-a-lifetime show."

This statement cut straight to the quick in Brandon's heart. It was true. He had been a jock of the theater stage while in high school and even on into college. Jake had only been in one play—and that was only because Brandon had been sick on opening night and was unable to perform. Jake acted his part by reading from the playbook while on stage. The audience loved it. It was so avant-garde! Jake was an immediate success, and Brandon was banned from theater forever.

"You're such a poor loser," Cynthia said.

"No, I'm not," Brandon replied, "and to prove it, I'm going to start my own talent show!"

The next two weeks proved to be utterly chaotic with Jake and Brandon competing with each other to sign people up for their individual talent shows. There was even a rumor going around that money was being offered to perform in these shows. Pretty soon, the whole town was divided into Jake's show and Brandon's show. The only problem was there was no one left to be in the audience. Jake, Maureen, Brandon, and Cynthia decided to get together and have a serious talk.

"Now, Brandon," Cynthia pleaded, "be reasonable. Do you really need the lion act in your show?"

"Hey, I found the act. It's one of a kind," Brandon protested. "Don't try to steal my headliner."

"Yeah, but I hear the guy has never worked with lions before," Jake added, "and, besides that, where are you going to get the lions?"

"Well, what about your elephant act?" Brandon retorted. "You know that the stage isn't even big enough for one elephant, much less ten!"

Maureen had enough of this infernal bickering. What started out as a great idea in her parlor to cheer up Laura turned into an event that pitted father against son and daughter against mother. Disgusted, Laura and Robert left the town and moved to the city. The whole sanitation department, gone with the wind! That was why the others were so snobby about seeing Laura and Robert at the club. Little did they know that they were actually world-renowned environmental scientists who came to their town to study their garbage and give them ideas on how to save hundreds, maybe even thousands, of dollars in recycling. Boo hoo, Maureen thought to herself.

BUT, Laura and Robert couldn't resist the idea of being in the talent show, showing off their old soft-shoe. After they had spent hundreds of dollars moving to the city, they spent thousands more moving back to their same old house. Maureen, when she found out that they were back, threw them a house warming party to beat the band. There was Jake in his mink stole, Brandon in his tour-de-tux, and Cynthia on the pipes with her chiffon blue formal. Laura and Robert were so taken back by the sudden show of affection that they broke out in tears.

"Speech, speech," everybody yelled.

"Wel l. . . " Robert said shyly, but egged on by Laura, he continued, "Ladies and Gentlemen, we are privileged to have such good friends, much less the fruit and dessert that accompany such an occasion. Delightful, delectable, and delicious are the very words to describe such a grandiose affair, a most sumptuous and palatable party."

Laura suddenly piped in her two cents worth.

"Where's the bathroom?"

Everyone clapped with polite smiles on their faces.

Suddenly, from out of nowhere, music began to play, and Laura and Robert suddenly started dancing.

"Hey, everybody, look at us," they sang. "You never used to give us the time of day or let us ride in the bus. But now that we are big time environmentalists, you all want to be just like us!"

"Yeah," said Laura clapping her hands.

Everyone started to dance, clapping their hands, and enjoying the affair immensely. Laura and Robert were their type of people, and they could use their country club facilities for as long as they wanted. Could too!

The next day, arbitration began again with Laura, Robert, Brandon, Jake, Cynthia, and Maureen working out all the details of who should be in the show, when dress rehearsals would be, where the show would be, and how much they should charge everyone who attended.

In fact, arbitration was going great until who should walk into the door but Marilyn—the woman Jake spent all night with at the Annual Riverside Gala Ball.

Maureen suddenly went pale.

Marilyn was a high society woman. She rarely associated with the likes of Jake except on those occasions when she wanted some free legal advice. However, on one particular occasion, although she had received free advice, she had fallen madly in love with Jake, something she had never dreamed about or expected. She had not heard from him in days and was so desperate to see him that she was willing to crash arbitration just to be with him one more time.

Suddenly, just as she sat down and let everyone stare at her in utter amazement and horror, the roof where they were meeting caved in and a brick fell promptly on each and everyone's head. Everyone, although a little dazed, continued on their meeting as though nothing had happened.

"TO BE OR NOT TO BE!" Jake said.

"Jake!" Maureen screamed. "Don't tell me that you are going to do Hamlet at the talent show?"

"Yes..." Jake said, "I am."

Everybody clapped.

"Bravo, jolly good idea, old chap," everyone said.

"And I," said Cynthia, "I am going to do Swan Lake."

"But," Maureen said, "you can't even dance!"

"I am a swan. Swans don't need to learn to dance," Cynthia said.

"Why . . . why, I guess you are right!" Maureen said. "One scene from Swan Lake coming right up."

"Who said anything about one scene?" Cynthia said. "I am going to do the entire Swan Lake!"

Everybody clapped.

"Yeah, like I said before," said Brandon, "who needs a lion act when you can have culture like a bunch of dogs walking back and forth across stage?"

"I'm going to show the audience how to dress Barbie up for a really cool date with Ken," Marilyn said.

"I'm going to walk around the stage with a big magnifying glass and look all around until I suddenly look out and see the audience and say 'I SEE YOU' with a big loud voice," Robert said.

"Boy, I can see it now," Laura said and just roared with laughter. Soon everyone was laughing.

"You know," said Maureen wiping the tears from her eyes, "with all this talent, who needs to sign up any riffraff? Why, we can do the show all ourselves!"

"Yeah, and forget all about the Civic Center," Jake said. "We'll have it exclusively at the Riverside Country Club where only members will be allowed the rare treat of catching a glimpse of our ravishing performances."

"And, at the end, we'll all throw big buckets of ice water into the audience!" Cynthia said to everyone's hearty agreement.

"A thousand dollars a ticket, too!" screamed Maureen and everyone screamed.

Unfortunately, my dear reader friends, the next two weeks were disastrous as far as ticket sales were concerned. No one was buying, not even Jake and Maureen's parents. Finally, in desperation, they lowered the ticket sales to $50 per person. Even so, the ticket sales were dismal. Finally, they started having contests to give the tickets away as prizes.

"Time for another call," Jake said as he reached for the phone. "Quick, give me an easy trivia question to ask!"

The phone rang several times before someone picked it up.

"Hello," a sultry voice answered.

Jake was totally taken aback by the beautiful voice. He could just imagine the beauty behind the voice. He almost forgot the question.

"Er-hello, madam," Jake replied, "could you tell me who was the first president of the United States?"

"Is this some sort of joke or something?" the woman asked in a slightly irritated tone of voice. "Everyone knows it was George Washington . . ."

Jake was delighted that she got it right! He yelled into the phone that she had answered correctly and had won the grand prize—two tickets to the talent show. The phone clicked before he had a chance to finish.

"Another person hung up," Jake muttered. "This isn't working. We should never have signed everyone up and then told them to take a hike."

Brandon shrugged his shoulders. At least he had been able to give away twenty tickets to his out of town friends.

"We need a miracle," he said.

After a long consultation with Maureen, Marilyn, Laura, Robert, and Cynthia, Jake and Brandon decided to bring in a bigwig PR person from New York to help them with their show.

"Hello, darlings," Antonio said as he tossed his coat on top of Jake's desk. He daintily plucked the cigarette holder out of his mouth and posed in front of Jake with one hand holding onto the holder and the other on his hip. He then sashayed around the room looking at all of Jake's civic awards.

Suddenly, he froze when he saw one of the awards. It was an award from the city to Jake's firm for putting away Scantonio Listerelli—Antonio's father!!!

"Oh yes," Antonio said, "I really do think that this show could use a little PR from the likes of me. First, everything must go. The stage, the costumes, the country club. . . "

"The. . . the country club?" Brandon asked.

"Yes, blow it up or something," he said. "I'm a gonna blow it up if you guys don't, see?"

Maureen was certain that Antonio had been smoking a cigarette a moment ago. Now, he had a big cigar, and he was puffing on it real good.

"Ya know what else we need?" he growled.

"No, what?" everybody asked.

"A DECENT FIVE-CENT CIGAR!" He screamed. Everyone immediately became frightened and wanted Antonio to leave.

"Oh... So you all want me to leave, do you?" he asked. "Well, you guys aren't going to get rid of me that easy! You hired me to do a job, and a job I'm a gonna do!"

"Now, now, Antonio," said Maureen, "let's not do anything hasty."

Antonio took out a knife and cut all the phone lines.

"BUT, we will never be able to sell any tickets now!" protested Jake.

"Oh, we will never be able to sell any tickets now," mimicked Antonio. "What do you take me for? A simpleton?"

No one dared to say a word.

"A penny a head," Antonio said.

"What?" everyone said.

"You heard me!" Antonio screamed. "Everybody who is anybody will be let in for a penny a head!"

"Excuse me for thinking," Cynthia protested, "but I don't think that a penny a head is wise, cost-effective planning, much less PR!"

SUDDENLY, a loose brick fell down off the ceiling and hit Mr. Antonio right on the head!

"Errrrrr... five million dollars a ticket!" he said gleefully clapping his hands. "Take it or leave it."

Everyone suddenly lost their high hopes and expectations in Antonio's PR skills.

"Uh... maybe you need to go back to New York City and think about it some more, and then, come and see us again," Maureen said.

"Okay," Antonio said, "and when I come back, expect to see five or six more tickets prices that I have thought up all by myself!"

Antonio left to everyone's great joy. Suddenly, the phone rang, and a small, squeaky voice left a message on their answering machine.

"Beware the Ides of March!" the voice rang out.

Maureen quickly looked at when they had scheduled their talent show. She began to laugh hysterically.

"Can you believe it?" she screamed. "We scheduled the show on the fifteenth of March. No wonder we haven't been able to sell any tickets!"

"Or even give them away!" Jake said.

"Let's do an experiment," Cynthia said and picked up the phone, dialed a number randomly and began a sales pitch the moment the person answered the phone.

"Wanna buy a pair of tickets to the Annual Gala Riverside Talent Show?" she asked. "It is on March sixteenth and not the fifteenth as originally planned."

"Sure," the voice said. "Why not? How much are they?"

"Uh ... Uh . . . Uh. . . " Cynthia said, suddenly blank, "uh. . . one penny!"

"Hey, great," the voice said. "I'll take a thousand."

"Wow," Cynthia said. "That's all we have! Wow, gee, great, thank you very much."

When she hung up the phone, Maureen was glaring at Cynthia. For all the thousands of dollars they had spent on advertising and preparation, Cynthia had sold all the tickets for a mere ten dollars.

"So! You just had to go and sell all the tickets for a miserable one penny apiece, did you?" Maureen hissed. "Do you know how many thousands of dollars we have spent just on advertising alone?"

Cynthia looked around the room for sympathy but there was none.

Jake, thinking how his law firm was going to cover 80% of the expenses, began to feverishly calculate in his mind how long it would take to revamp such a huge loss. He roughly estimated that in ten years, if his law firm was successful enough to win every case in court, they would just break even.

Brandon suddenly held up a severed telephone cord.

"Cynthia, you scream, you were talking into a dead phone all along!" he said.

Suddenly, everyone started laughing and skipping around.

"I'll put in another 80%!" Jake screamed and laughed.

Cynthia stood there dumbfounded. She was sure that she had talked with someone on the phone, but she was not sure how. Perhaps, she thought, she was going crazy.

Suddenly, she heard the voice again. Everyone looked around the room to see who had spoken. No one could see anything, but they all heard a small voice.

Suddenly, Marilyn began laughing and laughing.

"I can throw my voice," she said. "I fooled you. I sure did."

Everyone howled! Marilyn was such a scream. Maureen went right up to her face and screamed as loud as she could. Everyone laughed and laughed. It was a good day. Everybody was having fun.

"You know," Jake said to Maureen, "if everything works out, you and I are going to get married."

"OH JAKE, OH JAKE!" Maureen said.

"If they get married, you and I are going on our second honeymoon," Brandon told Cynthia.

Cynthia held up a big sign that she had quickly worked up:

Cynthia B. Williams live on stage—Swan Lake— and billions and billions of swans

"Quack, quack!" Brandon said.

"Now, don't think me mad, Brandon," she said, "but I am going to fulfill my lifelong dream of being a professional tap dancer. No second honeymoon must come between me and my goal."

"Tap dancing?" Brandon said. "Swan Lake is a ballet—not a tap dance!"

Cynthia began to cry.

Maureen comforted her.

"Listen, kid," she said, "if you want to tap dance out Swan Lake, go right ahead and do it. No one will try to stop you."

"I am such a fraud," Cynthia said. "It's true! Brandon is right.

I never could dance. I didn't even know that Swan Lake was a ballet until now. You see how stupid I am!"

Cynthia stopped talking and looked around. Her voice was still going on and on.

". . . Yes, I am such a fraud. I can't sing either. In fact, I can't do anything! Ask Brandon. I can't cook, I can't clean, I can't even use the remote control for the TV!"

"Marilyn," everyone screamed. Even Cynthia started laughing.

"I guess that means my ventriloquist act is in the show, huh?" Marilyn replied without moving her lips.

"Now, you guys all know that it wasn't me who said that I didn't even know that Swan Lake was a ballet until now. In fact, before I came here, I graduated from Julliard and had a short career with the Metropolitan Ballet Company until I got pregnant," Cynthia added.

Everyone was stunned and looked at Brandon who was absolutely speechless. Pregnant?

But, he and Cynthia were childless! And, he had no idea that his wife even knew how to dance, much less be a ballerina!

Then, to everyone's surprise, Cynthia got up on her toes and pirouetted around the room. It was beautiful!

Maureen had to break the silence before Brandon cracked up, "Cynthia, darling. Pregnant? What happened to the baby? And who was the father?"

Cynthia stopped spinning and sat gracefully on the nearest chair.

"I gave it up for adoption. He should be about 30 years old now. His father was a very promising dancer before he was killed in a fall from the stage during a performance. We were supposed to get married."

Suddenly, Laura screamed out, "My brother Philip was in an accident like that 30 years ago! But he didn't die, he was just paralyzed."

Cynthia couldn't believe what she was hearing.

"Your brother, is his name Philip Mark Andrews?" she asked hesitantly.

"Yes," Laura answered, "I have a different last name because I changed my name during my short stint as a dancer."

Cynthia fell on Laura's shoulder and began to sob uncontrollably.

"You're Philip's little sister Laurie. He told me so much about you," Cynthia cried. "They all told me that he was dead. I didn't know, I didn't know. . . "

Cynthia collapsed in a chair, and Maureen quickly brought her a glass of water.

"How is Philip?" Cynthia asked, wiping the tears from her face. "Where is he, how is he doing?"

"He's fine, but he still can't walk," Laura replied. "You know, a young man keeps coming to visit him, but Philip won't tell me who he is. He showed up at Philip's doorstep about five years ago. He looks like he's about 30 years old. I wonder if he's your son."

Cynthia again noticed that she was just moving her lips and not really saying all this. Laura, too, was not speaking. It was as if a mysterious force were pulling a string on their backs and making their mouths move.

Cynthia and Laura looked at Marilyn. She had her hands over her mouth. She was trying her best not to laugh. Suddenly, she just couldn't help it. She laughed out loud, and Cynthia and Laura had to laugh with her. Cynthia got up to pirouette again and fell right into the brick wall.

"I told you I was such a klutz!" She screamed and laughed.

Maureen woke with a start. She had dozed off with the newspaper in her hand. Laura and Robert's grinning faces still smiled at her from the front of the society section. Grrr, Maureen thought, I'll get even with them. She felt like she had had the funniest dream. Something about a talent show. The dream had everyone in it, even Laura and Robert and Jake's old girlfriend, Marilyn. Maureen shrugged her shoulders and sat down at her vanity table to brush her long blond hair. She suddenly felt very sorry that she was going to break her engagement with Jake. She wished she had gone to the Ball with him just this one last time so that she could have one last pleasant memory of him.

Suddenly, she woke with a start again. She looked around the room. Everyone was calling her name, but it wasn't "Maureen." They were calling her something else. They were calling her "Cynthia."

"Ouch, my head," Cynthia said.

"You had a nasty hit after you danced into that wall," Brandon said and then looked around to see if he was saying that or if Marilyn was throwing her voice again.

Maureen clapped her hands.

"Okay, enough of this nonsense," she said. "We need to get our talent show finalized and on the road. We only have a week to go, you know."

The night of the big talent show finally arrived. They were sold out. They even sold the tickets for $100 apiece, more than covering their expenses. Everyone gathered backstage for a pep talk before going on. Jake looked splendid in his MC tuxedo. Cynthia's tap dancing adaptation of Swan Lake was absolutely divine, reminiscent of Fred Aster and Ginger Spice. Suddenly, there was a commotion at the back door.

"Good gosh, it's Antonio," Jake exclaimed.

"Gotta dance! Gotta sing!" Antonio said, and, throwing off his coat, he stood in a dazzling rhinestone outfit with a rhinestone cane.

"Er . . . " Jake said dumbfounded.

Antonio pushed him aside and went out onto the stage.

"Welcome to my show, Ladies and Gentlemen!" he said and bowed graciously with his baton between his arm and his torso. The whole audience applauded loudly.

"You. . . you can't do this!" Jake protested. "I'm the MC!"

Cynthia, who had started to practice her tap dancing before the show began, started to tap a little harder since all the commotion was making her nervous.

"TIPPY TAP, TIPPY TAP," her little shoes went.

Maureen and Marilyn went home. They went in a big car. The car was red. It went very fast. They were making cookies. They were making brown cookies. They were going to eat the cookies.

See Laura. See Laura and Robert. See Laura and Robert standing around watching the show. See the audience laughing. They are laughing at Antonio. He is very, very funny. They laugh and laugh and laugh. Laura and Robert are laughing, too.

See Jake. See Jake laugh and laugh. See Jake jump and dance. He is mad. He has gone mad.

Antonio is funny. He is very funny.

"Get out there and dance!" Jake suddenly screamed pulling at Cynthia's outfit.

"No, Jake, no," Cynthia screamed. "I am not ready now. I am not even suppose to be on."

"You'll go on stage when I say you go on stage!" Jake screamed and laughed and then threw Cynthia onto the stage.

Antonio was amazed that Swan Lake was starting even before he had a chance to announce it.

He started to tap dance. Cynthia couldn't believe that he was trying to steal her act.

"Ha-ha," Jake said. "From bad to worse. This whole stinking talent show has just gone down the drain. He's a tough cookie to follow. Wanna try it Cynthia? Huh?"

"No!" Cynthia screamed. "It's not happening. This is a nightmare. This is not the way we rehearsed it. This is not what we planned!"

Moral of this story?

Look before you tap!

The End

THE LOST CHRISTMAS PARTY

Joe's hands trembled as he took the large glass of bourbon.

"I really need this. I can't play Santa any other way."

David looked at him with disgust, and then, David looked at himself in the mirror in disgust. How in the world did he ever elect to choose Joe for Santa? Joe was a problem drinker. He knew that. Joe saw bats in the air and bugs crawling on the walls—and Joe had missed his last AA meeting!

"I need just another shot of bourbon," Joe said his body shaking and his face trembling with sweat. David watched him down a full glass of bourbon and then another and then another.

"If I can't play Santa Claus now, I never will!" Joe said and stood up, bracing himself on the table. "Let's go get dressed up!"

David helped Joe to the office where they were going to put on the elaborate costume that the company had paid $150 for. Joe ran into a wall and then another as David was leading him quite roughly to the changing room.

"I can't believe you're drunk! You are supposed to be playing Santa Claus for little children!"

"I'm not drunk. Them's fighting words," Joe said and took a swing at David. He missed and hit himself instead.

Cuckoo!

Joe fell down flat.

David shook him, but it was to no avail. Joe was out for the night.

"I can't believe this! I can't play Santa Claus!" David said to himself, but he saw the writing on the wall. He walked into the changing room and unwrapped the suit. The suit had been at Joe's house, and Joe had altered it to make it fit.

David pulled out the red coat. His eyes popped out of his head. There was bourbon stains on the red coat. He pulled out the pants. They had been cut at the knees. The red hat had sleigh bells stapled to hang down the sides like dread locks. There was no beard, but only a piece of paper that had been cut out to resemble a small Van-Dyke. The black belt was Joe's white Karate belt (Joe had never gotten very far in his Karate classes).

"No!"

David could hear the children in the next room. They were all excited. Santa was coming. It was going to be a magical evening. David walked around the room several times. He wondered what in the world he could do at the last moment. He kept walking around and around. Suddenly, he stepped on a small thumbtack.

"Ouch!" David screamed. He lost his balance and fell backward hitting his head against the office desk.

When David sat up he saw the world as he had never seen it before. Yes! This was a magical evening, and Santa Claus was going to go in nouveau chic clothes with magic tricks up his sleeve.

"I am the Magic Santa Claus!" David said and clapped his hands. The beard easily super glued to his face. He took a dark pencil and painted bags under his eyes and made his eyebrows sharp and mean. He looked into the mirror and waved his white sequined gloves.

"It's show time, folks!"

David quickly grabbed a few props for his magic tricks from the office and ran outside. In a few minutes, he would enter the building as the coolest Santa in history. He even sported a nice set of pink-tinted granny glasses.

Instead of the usual "Ho-ho-ho," David entered the building bellowing out, "Peace, Love, Dove!"

The children and their parents suddenly stopped their festive mirth and stared at the creature that had entered into the building. Some of the smaller children began to cry and clutched onto their parent's legs. Of all the people, David's wife was more stunned than any.

"Well, presto, abracadabra!" David screamed. "I've got a million tricks, ladies and gentlemen, and they are all up my sleeves!"

"David!" David's wife harshly whispered, coming up to him.

"Well, so quickly a volunteer!" David said. "Now you see her, now you don't!"

David pushed his wife into the Christmas tree where she fell backward, and the tree collapsed on top of her. Her husband was definitely on her list now.

"Tah-dah!" David said and laughed.

David took a glass of water from a nearby table and went up to the head of the company.

"Been a good boy this past year?" he asked. The head of the company didn't say a word.

"You see the water in this glass?"

The director, seeing what was coming, quickly ducked under the table, but he was not quick enough since David poured the water on his head just as he was going down. David was on his list, too!

"Tah-dah! I must be a pessimist. It was full. Now it's empty!"

A few of the men tried to wrestle David to the ground, but David was too strong and threw them clear across the room. He overthrew some tables and shouted at them:

"Bring it!"

The sleigh bells on his head frantically rang out as David grabbed some presents and called out the names as quickly as possible before throwing them full force at the children. Fortunately, the parents sheltered their little precious ones. David was on their Christmas list now. In fact, David was on everyone's list!

Ho! Ho! Ho!

The End

A WALK IN THE WOODS

It was a beautiful spring day. Susan had woken up early this morning, not willing to waste one minute of the first day of her spring vacation. Her classes had been particularly difficult this semester, and she was looking forward to a week without books, or lectures, or studying.

She pulled a sweatshirt over her head and brushed her long blonde hair. She walked into the kitchen and kissed her mother on the cheek.

"Why, hello, Susan," her mother exclaimed. "You're up early this morning!"

Susan smiled as she grabbed a blueberry muffin off the table.

"I just want to enjoy my vacation, that's all," she replied. "I'll eat breakfast when I get back. I'm going for a walk in the woods."

Suddenly, there was a knock at the door. It was Frank. Susan could see him smiling and waving to her from the outside window. Her heart jumped at the sight of her love.

"Oh, Frank! Frank!" she cried and ran to let her love in.

"Susan, I want you to run across town and right now!"

"Whatever you say," Susan said and began to run.

Frank watched her disappear over the horizon.

"There. That should do it," he said and laughed. "The blueberry muffins will be all mine now."

Frank knocked on the door and Mrs. Snyder looked up from her busyness and told Frank to get on in there. Frank eagerly came in and saw the blueberry muffins.

"May I have one, Mrs. Snyder?" Frank asked.

"Of course you may, dear, please help yourself."

Frank eagerly began to eat the muffins, stuffing as many as he could into his mouth. He could barely talk much less swallow.

Susan stopped running, breathless, and sat by the road. What was she doing there, she wondered? One minute, she was going for a walk in the woods, and the next minute, she was going for a world record in the 100-yard dash! She slowly made her way back to the house. As she neared her house, she could see Frank's car in the driveway. Her heart sank. She had meant to invite Frank over and tell him that it was over between the two of them. The control that he exerted over her life was too consuming, too overpowering. It was actually his presence that had contributed to the difficulty that she had experienced last semester. But, it was too early in the morning for a confrontation.

Susan stopped walking towards the house and headed for the woods. The air was cool and crisp, and she could hear a bird chirping in the distance. A light breeze ruffled through her hair, and the slightly damp grass cushioned her footsteps as she paced forward. The house soon dropped out of sight, and it was just Susan, Susan and her lovely woods.

Suddenly, she came upon a young man bent over something on the ground.

"Land sakes! You have gobbled all those muffins down," Mrs. Snyder said.

"Wow, Mrs. Snyder. I love muffins. Do you have anything else to eat?"

"My, my. To be young again," Mrs. Snyder said laughing. "Would you care for me to whip you up some bacon and eggs?"

"Sure, Mrs. Snyder, and biscuits, too!"

Mrs. Snyder began to cook for Frank while Frank looked outside. Susan was nowhere to be seen.

"Good," he thought, "she is a real stinkeroo!"

Mrs. Snyder stopped her work.

"Frank? Could you please be a dear and get me that pan over there?"

Frank got up and reached for a brass pot over the sink.

"Is this the one?" he asked.

"Sure is, honey," Mrs. Snyder said with a smile. "Anything else you would like me to cook for you while you are here, sweetie?"

"Tea. . . and coffee," Frank said trying to act grown-up for all grown-ups he had seen drank either tea or coffee. Frank would show Mrs. Snyder that he was R-E-A-L-L-Y grown-up by imbibing both beverages.

Mrs. Snyder frowned as she took out the coffee and the tea bags from the kitchen cupboard. She was a practical woman, and she didn't like serving someone both coffee and tea when it wasn't necessary.

"Oh, Frank, are you sure you want both coffee AND tea," she asked.

"Sure, Mrs. Snyder," Frank replied, "and some freshly squeezed orange juice, too. Oh, do you have any mango juice? I just love mango juice!"

Mrs. Snyder had never heard such rubbish in all her life. But, being the good hostess that she always was, she put the kettle on the stove. Pretty soon, it was whistling a happy tune.

"Hello," Susan said tentatively, "what are you looking at?"

The young man looked up at her with the bluest eyes that she had ever seen. In his hand, he held a tiny baby bird.

"I think this little fellow fell out of his nest," he explained. "I really don't know what to do with him."

Susan's heart pounded as she gazed into his eyes. He ran his other hand through his black curly hair, a little tousled by the wind, with a slight tinge of self-consciousness.

"Oh, you can't put it back in its nest, assuming you can find it," she said. "The mother bird will never accept it back now that you've touched it."

The young man looked surprised and then remorseful as he realized that his lack of knowledge had forever separated the little bird from his mother.

"Fool!" the man said to the little bird. "Why did you torment me so with your beautiful singing that I was forced to pry you from your nest? You have deprived yourself of your very life!"

"Oh, I don't think it is all that bad," Susan said putting her hand on his shoulder. "Millions of birds fall out nests every year and die. Why should you fret yourself that this bird wouldn't have done the same?"

"I'm sorry. Was I being that melodramatic?" The young man said. "I am sorry to have brought it up."

"No, no. Please express yourself."

"Okay. Watch this," the man said, taking the bird and throwing it as far as it could go. The small bird pitifully flapped its wings before taking a free fall to the raging river below. Susan was shocked.

"I'll have prune juice and apple juice and pear juice and carrot juice . . . " Frank said.

"Yes . . . yes . . . yes . . . yes . . . " Mrs. Snyder was saying like a robot opening up the icebox, putting vegetables and fruits in the juice extractor and juggling two hot pots of tea and coffee.

"OHHH, I have to go to the bathroom," Frank moaned as he downed the last glass of prune juice. Holding his stomach, he raced to the hall bathroom while Mrs. Snyder looked on.

"What about the coffee!" she yelled after him.

Susan screamed and ran towards the river. The young man raced after her.

"The bird, I have to save the bird," she sobbed.

They found the bird on the bank of the river. Susan cradled in her hand. It would never sing another song. It would never soar to new heights. It would never see another day.

"I-I'm s-sorry," the young man stammered, "I-I'm from the city. I thought all birds knew how to fly. I didn't know it couldn't fly. I really didn't!"

He reached down to help her up from the river's edge.

Susan collapsed into his arms and sobbed against his chest.

Life was such a fragile thing. So unpredictable, so cruel.

The young man held her close to his heart. He didn't know what had brought him to the woods this morning. He was a reporter from the city and was sent here to do a story on the natural wildlife in these woods. Now, unexpectedly, he was holding a beautiful woman in his arms, and he didn't even know her name.

"My name is John. What's your name?" he asked.

"Why do you ask? Seeing that it is Bitter!" Susan cried.

"Bitter?" John asked. "I had never heard of a girl called Bitter. Pleased to meet you, Bitter."

"No!" Susan shouted and pushed herself away from this stranger. "You don't know a thing, do you?! I want to leave now."

"No one is stopping you, Bitter," the reporter said and then pulled out a camera. "Mind if I snap a picture before you leave?"

Susan looked around. It was getting cold. The day was not turning out as she had planned. Were all men so cruel?

"Say Cheese!" John said and snapped the picture.

Susan stood stunned for a moment and then quickly turned and ran deeper into the woods. She would never talk to men again. Never!

Mrs. Snyder knocked on the door holding a tray of freshly baked cookies.

"Frank? Frank? Are you alright in there? I have some chocolate chip cookies. Come out and eat them before they get cold."

Frank threw up again. He couldn't believe he had eaten so much. Wouldn't Mrs. Snyder ever leave him alone?

Frank was feeling better and got up to flush the toilet. It wouldn't flush. The handle was broken. Frank panicked. He couldn't leave the bathroom like this! He decided to go out the bathroom window.

Mrs. Snyder was getting concerned. Frank had been in the bathroom for over an hour now, and the delicious lasagna that she had baked for him was getting cold. Her soufflé was ready to collapse. Mrs. Snyder began to cry quietly to herself, wringing her apron.

Frank ran towards the woods as fast as possible. He had to get away from that house of culinary horror as fast as he could.

"Smile, you're on the front page!" someone shouted as he stumbled through the underbrush. A young man snapped his picture. The flash momentarily blinded Frank, and he lunged for his unseen assailant. They wrestled on the ground.

"Stop, stop, the both of you," Susan screamed, "I'm not worth fighting over!"

The two men stopped fighting immediately. They both looked at Susan.

Susan ran deeper into the woods again. The Super Sports trials would be in two months. She had to get into shape. She had high hopes for her chances in cross-country running. The thought of her marching behind the U.S. Flag in her cute red, white, and blue Super Sports uniform sent shivers up and down her spine.

The cherry pie Mrs. Snyder had baked sent a golden scent wafting throughout the meadows where the two men were both wonderfully surprised at the sight of Susan and then woeful at her leaving and then waxing whimsical at the sight of Susan again with a bird's nest in her hand.

"I'm going to make soup. Anyone want to join me?" she said with a wink, and then she ran to her house.

Mrs. Snyder came outside to look for Frank after she had taken the bathroom door off and had given the bathroom a good scrubbing. He had forgotten to take some cupcakes home to his mother. She saw Susan running toward the house. She quickly took out a stopwatch.

"Hurry up, Susan! You can beat your time! Run child! Run!"

Susan quickly ran past her mother who clapped her hands in glee.

"World record!" she screamed and jumped for joy. Her daughter was going to be in the Super Sports for sure!

Mrs. Snyder waved to the two men to come into the house. The two men hesitated, but the smell of the cherry pie beckoned them. Reluctantly, they walked towards the house.

Mrs. Snyder, John, and Frank were all sitting around the kitchen table, eating cherry pie with fresh whipped cream and drinking coffee and tea and twelve different types of fruit juices when Susan appeared, straight from the shower. She had on a pretty pink bathrobe and a towel wrapped around her head like a sultan.

Mrs. Snyder turned to the stove and stirred the collard greens. She opened her oven and observed that the cornbread was turning out quite nicely.

"And Susan? Once you get your clothes on, run across town again!" Frank yelled after her.

"Yeah! Take a hike!" John said with a smile and then took another sip of papaya juice.

Within minutes, the screen door was once again opened and slammed, and Susan was off like a flash, raising dust as she ran toward the horizon and once again disappeared. Mrs. Snyder pressed her face against the kitchen window.

"Land Sakes! Doesn't that girl ever want to eat?"

At that very moment, a limousine drove up to the Snyder's home and a tall, young, handsome man with brown, wavy hair and sea-green eyes stepped out of the car. Mrs. Snyder could see that he had the Super Sports insignia on his shirt.

"Can it be? Can it really be?" she cried and ran to the door.

"Hello, ma'am," the man said. "I am with the Super Sports Search Committee and I have heard your daughter is quite a runner. Could I please talk with her and with you?"

"Well, you get right in here and have some coffee. Susan—my daughter—is out practicing right now. She should be running back any minute now."

At that moment, Susan came running up. The towel had fallen off her head and her beautiful long blonde hair shone in the sunlight. She was amazed to see the fancy car in the driveway. It was the very first elegant automobile that she had ever seen in her driveway.

"Susan! You'll never believe who this is!" Mrs. Snyder yelled. "He's come all the way from Washington, D.C.!"

"Well, no, actually . . . " the man squirmed. "I never said that I'm from Washington. I'm actually from the next town."

Susan was mortified that she was standing there in just her pretty little chiffon paisley dress. She quickly ducked inside the house to get dressed.

"She'll be out shortly," Mrs. Snyder said apologetically. "Please step inside my kitchen."

The warm aroma of cherry pie and baking cornbread greeted the man as he entered the kitchen. He was surprised to see two other men sitting at the table, eating pie and drinking coffee.

"Oh, I see you have company," he said. "Shall I come at another time?"

"Nonsense," Mrs. Snyder replied. "These boys aren't company. In fact, they're not even important. Now, you just set yourself down and have some of my famous cherry pie."

John took out a note pad and began to feverishly jot down some notes.

"What is your recipe for this delicious cherry pie, Mrs. Snyder," he inquired.

As he got the ingredients and the directions from Mrs. Snyder, Frank and the man struck up a conversation.

"So, you here to court Susan, too?" he asked.

The man was completely taken aback. Mind you, Susan was a beautiful girl and a delight to behold. Any fool would be glad to accept her hand in marriage. However, he had just gotten there and hadn't even been introduced to her.

"Uh, nooo . . ." he ventured, "I'm from the Super Sports Search Committee. I'm here to see just how good a runner Susan really is."

Frank jumped up from the table and did several back flips in a roll. This took everyone by surprise, and Mrs. Snyder dropped the cornbread that she was taking out of the oven.

"I'm a champion gymnast!" Frank yelled. "Watch me, watch me . . ."

At that moment, Jim drove up in his convertible and honked his horn. Mrs. Snyder dropped the collard greens.

"My word! What is that boy doing here now?"

Jim let his long, strawberry blonde hair blow in the breeze. He was wearing silver shades and was sporting the finest clothes of any rich boy in the county.

Susan and he had talked about marriage, but they were not serious until their telephone call the night before. After expressing their love for one another for the umpteenth time, Jim finally decided it was time to drop the question.

"Hey, Mrs. Snyder," Jim yelled, "is Susan in? Tell her to come out."

Mrs. Snyder frowned. Just when Susan was being given her big chance to do something she had dreamed of all her life, Jim had to come and demand that she come and sit with him for a while.

"Very well," Mrs. Snyder said, "I'll send her out right away. Susan? Jim is here!"

A crash of a windowpane was heard, and Mrs. Snyder saw Susan fall to the ground below.

"Susan? Are you alright!" Mrs. Snyder screamed.

"Jim! Jim! My love!" Susan said. "Why have you been so late getting here?"

"Had to get up my nerve," Jim said.

"Nerve?" Susan nervously asked. "Why?"

"Susan...I...I know this is awkward and probably not the right place or time, but... Susan... uh... " Jim said, "would you marry me?"

Right then, little Tommy Jones, from across the street, was trying to hit a small tin can with a rock, when his aim was too high and instead of hitting the can, landed the stone square dab on top of Susan's beautiful head.

"Ouch!" Susan said and then looked at Jim with a strange, quizzical look. "You haven't seen me jump yet, have you, my dear?"

Jim was taken back by this sudden change of conversation. "What?"

"I can jump over your car, Jim dear," Susan said. She quickly ran and jumped. Her leg hit the side view mirror, and a snapping noise was clearly heard.

"SUSAN!" Mrs. Snyder suddenly screamed. Jim jumped up and started climbing out over the rear end of his car. Frank hastily stuffed a few more hard-boiled eggs in his pocket and ran out. John quickly snapped a picture while the man from the Super Sports Committee took out a pencil and crossed Susan's name off the list. Little Tommy, seeing Susan on the floor and knowing that his rock had hit her pretty little head suddenly began to cry.

"I'm sorry! I'm sorry!" he began to bawl. "Give me one more chance!"

"Jim, my love!" Susan screamed.

"You will be alright, my sweet. Don't fret. Don't cry. I love you. I really love you!"

Susan sobbed hysterically. Little Tommy came near her and began to bawl uncontrollably.

"Give me one more chance!"

Mrs. Snyder took Susan and helped her to her feet.

"Never do that again!" she said. "You gave me such a scare."

Yes. It was true. There, lying on the ground, was a broken side view mirror. It had snapped clean off Jim's car, but Jim was more concerned with his true love's fall.

"You didn't hurt one little bone of your precious little body, did you?" Jim pleaded, and the pleas did not fall on deaf ears for Susan blew him a kiss.

Frank had hard-boiled eggs sticking out of his mouth. He ran over to Susan, and she began to laugh. First, she shook a little, then she shook a lot, and finally she bellowed one great, big guffaw, and everyone laughed with her.

"Frank! You. . . you. . . Frank, you!" Susan screamed.

Suddenly, to everyone's surprise, little Tommy leaped on Susan and gave her a great big kiss on the mouth.

"Why . . . why . . . Tommy," Susan stammered, "where did a twelve-year old boy like you learn to kiss like that?"

Little Tommy gave her a wink and said, "From the movies, of course. Oh Susan, I've been in love with you ever since you started baby-sitting me when I was four!"

Susan couldn't believe what she was hearing. She always thought little Tommy was cute, but now, she was seeing him in a different light. Why should she marry Jim who was incredibly handsome and filthy rich? Why should she wed Frank who loved her with a passion unheard-of? Why should she become the wife of John, a man probably headed for some fancy journalism award? Why should she accept the proposal of the Super Sports Committee and therefore fulfill her lifelong dream? No, now there was only little Tommy. She would probably have to adopt him first and then wait till he was eighteen to make him her husband.

"Tommy! I had no idea! Do you have a job," Susan asked.

"I have a paper route everyday, before school starts," Tommy replied.

"Perfect," Susan said. "Do you have a house?"

"Well, I have a tree house in our yard," Tommy ventured.

"Perfect," Susan said. "How about wheels?"

"Um, I have a radio flyer," replied Tommy. "It goes really fast, too!"

Susan flung her arms around Tommy's neck. "You're the guy of my dreams. Let's get married in 6 years!"

It was the happiest day of little Tommy's life, but Mrs. Snyder would have nothing to do with it.

"March yourself right into the house this instance, young lady!" she screamed. Susan desperately looked up to see if her mother would give any indication that she was joking, but it was to no avail. She looked around at the other men who looked back at her with great bewilderment and confusion of heart.

"I will not only march, mother, I will skip, too!" Susan said gaily and then skipped happily to the house singing a nursery rhyme. Mrs. Snyder looked at her and inwardly felt grief. Oh, how she had wanted Susan to grow up. She had wanted her little girl to be normal—to be like the rest of the young teenagers. But Susan was too young at heart to realize the folly of her ways. She was too much like gelatin to ever be molded into anything that would retain its shape after one eating. She was a blubbering blob of mold—fungus, mildew, and yeast, too!

Mrs. Snyder looked around with embarrassment.

"I'm sorry. Please forgive me. I tried to raise her properly. I really did."

Suddenly, she broke down and began to cry. Jim came over and put his arm around her. Frank held her hand. John held her other hand. Tommy put his arms around her legs. Jack stroked her hair. Larry spoke with her with comfort.

"It's okay. Don't worry about this. Susan will come around. You will see."

Mrs. Snyder stared at the men around her.

"Want some pie?"

The men suddenly ran to the house.

"Me first! No, me!"

"I think you're just a horrible bunch of people," Susan screamed, coming down the stairs with a suitcase. "You've never accepted me. I was just a convenient doll to dress up! Well, I'm sick of it all. Sick of the way you go around doing things. You may find it amusing, but it makes me sick! I'm leaving and never coming back."

Someone had turned on the radio, and the old tune "Bye-bye Baby" engulfed the kitchen where Mrs. Snyder and all the pie devouring pigs sat, still and stunned. They heard the front screen door shut. Mrs. Snyder suddenly jumped up on her feet and ran to the front door.

"Susan! Susan!"

Susan stopped. She turned around.

"Yes, mother?"

A pie hit her full force in the face.

"Here's one for the road!"

The End

THE DINNER DATE

Frank was all prepared for Charesa that evening. He had gone to elaborate lengths to impress her with his cooking. There was not a stone left unturned in pleasing his date. Besides, nothing was too good for Charesa, the love of his life. Although she probably didn't understand his passionate feelings for her, Frank believed that she would be able to catch a glimpse of his love by his lavish setup.

Frank looked to see that the expensive china was well in order, the gold-plated silverware was polished and the crystal glasses spot free. His silken tablecloth was neatly placed on the well-polished, brand-new, dining room table underneath which lay a highly-prized Oriental rug. The candles were in handblown Italian holders. The vintage wine was in a disposable paper ice bucket.

In the kitchen, Frank made sure the lobster, Baked Alaska, Cherries Jubilee, freshly baked ham, Caesar salad, homemade ox tail soup, and petite carrots were all in tip-top condition. There was even a rack of goat embellished on a tray of Middle Eastern rice. The caviar and imported goat cheese were ready for the palate. The chopped liver was a must, and the cheese fondue was a sight for sore eyes. The orange, slushy drink was for later on in the evening. There was even a pink, slimy goo, which was Frank's own special creation.

The doorbell rang, and Frank, after adjusting his tuxedo, went merrily to the door.

Charesa nervously glanced into the hall mirror before ringing the doorbell. She hoped Frank would like the stunning red, satin evening gown that she had bought for this occasion. Her beautiful, black hair cascaded in rivers of curls down her back. Her ruby lips curled into a slight smile as she thought about Frank's reaction at the sight that would greet him when he opened the door. Up to now, Frank had only seen her in t-shirts and jeans with her hair in pigtails. This would be the first time he would see her in a dress and wearing make-up.

Charesa daintily lifted her dress and pushed the doorbell.

Frank opened the door and stood in a pleasingly stunned silence. Finally, he held up an orange, slushy drink and said:

"Would you care for a drink?"

Charesa didn't know what to say. His reaction to her outfit was disappointing to say the least, and she was wary of the drink, which was being offered to her. But, in the name of good manners, she accepted it and took a sip. It was straight vodka with orange food coloring! It was like drinking rubbing alcohol straight out of the bottle. Charesa felt sick to her stomach and tried to hold the rest of the liquid in her mouth. She wanted to ask Frank where the bathroom was so that she could discreetly throw the rest of the drink away and rinse her mouth.

"Er, um, where, um, bath, um," she struggled to say through the drink.

Frank beckoned her into the living room, ignoring her mumbling.

"Man, was my day at the office tiring," he said with orange teeth and an orange tongue. "I don't know how many files I had to complete. Please be seated, Charesa. Like I said, my day was really tiring, and my boss was after me all day to hurry up my work. Like, real fast, if you know what I mean. Say, that sure is a cheap outfit you're wearing, Charesa. How did you know that red was my favorite color?"

Charesa wished Frank would shut up. His incessant rambling was giving her a headache, and she couldn't hold the drink in her mouth any longer and had to swallow it. It hit the bottom of her stomach like a ton of bricks. Feeling light-headed, she smiled broadly at Frank and looked around the room.

"I love it, I love your orange teeth, I love your orange tongue, I love your day at work, and your boss, and my outfit, and what's this lovely pink stuff?!!" Charesa said.

Frank looked at her with a fake, orange smile. He let a little orange dribble come out and immediately sucked it up. He did it several times to try to impress her with his witty behavior.

"Say, Charesa," Frank said, "you sure look stunning tonight, my love. Ha-ha. Only kidding."

Drinking on an empty stomach made Charesa so very happy. She laughed at everything Frank was saying. She decided that she would impress him with her sense of humor, too, and put a spoonful of the pink, slimy stuff in her mouth.

"Look at me Frank, my love," she said. "I am a big, pink water fountain!"

With that, she spit the pink stuff all over Frank's ceiling.

When Frank looked up, the pink, slimy goo fell on top of his face. He politely laughed and wiped his face with Charesa's cascading hair with its rivers of curls.

"Ha-ha," Frank said. He now knew it was time to quit the silly business and get right down to his presentation of the engagement ring in his pocket.

"Charesa," he said solemnly, falling to his knees and taking her hand, "I have something very dear I would like to ask you."

"Grrr! Grrr!" Charesa snarled, holding her hands high over her head. "Look at me! Do you know what type of animal I am? Grrr! Grrr!"

Frank looked at her with a surprised look.

Charesa broke out into a laugh.

"I'm a grizzly bear!" Charesa said.

Frank suddenly didn't feel it appropriate to present the quarter-carat cubic zirconium ring to her until the evening was a little more spent. Besides, he thought, it would give her a chance to sober up a bit. A little food in her stomach might help.

Frank rose to his feet.

"Listen," he told her, "it's time to eat!"

Charesa had sobered up a bit in the past few minutes and was wondering what she had said and done since she drank some of that orange, slushy drink.

Frank looked at Charesa and pulled out a fiddle.

"Grab your pardners!" he said and started to fiddle madly.

Charesa had no choice but to dance frantically with invisible partners.

"Do-se-do, and around you go," Frank said and Charesa went around the couch.

"Pick up the pink goo and fling it in your shoe," Frank said and fiddled faster.

Charesa did exactly what he said and started dancing out of control, jumping up and down and falling down on the couch every minute or so, shaking her legs.

"Yee-haaa," she screamed.

The orange, slushy drink had apparently not worn off for both Frank and Charesa.

Frank threw his fiddle down.

"You wanna see my $300 water filter system in my kitchen?" he asked.

Charesa got up from the couch and clapped her hands.

"Ooooo," she cooed, "a genuine water filter system?"

They both ran to the kitchen, fighting to get through the narrow kitchen door. Frank showed her the water filter system and explained to her in technical terms how it all worked. Charesa stared dreamily at Frank as he spouted out one technical term after another.

"Oooooo," she said, "I can see why you bought it."

Frank turned on the faucet and filled a dirty glass.

"You see how dirty it is?" he asked.

"It sure is," she said. "It must be broke or something."

Frank then took a clean glass and filled it to overflowing so that water splashed all over the kitchen floor when he held it up to Charesa's face.

"Now," he said, "you see how clean it is?"

"Amazing," she said. "It absolutely positively works! I want one, too!"

"Let's get my money's worth," Frank said. "Let's fill up all my glasses. I even bought a new box of glasses today—the finest crystal one can buy."

"Can we do some more square dancing later?" Charesa asked.

Frank looked at her with great delight. She was really his type of dinner date. Charesa was really a fun gal.

"After dessert," he said with a smile.

"No, right now!" Charesa demanded, so Frank ran to get his fiddle. Charesa started to dance in anticipation of Frank's famous fiddling. Suddenly, Frank appeared at the entrance to the kitchen and held up his fiddle and bow.

"Tah-dah!" he screamed and started to fiddle madly, even foaming a little at the mouth.

Charesa got totally out of control, took the goat off the Middle Eastern rice platter, and started to dance with it. Frank just laughed and played louder and faster.

"Here," she said, "let me fiddle for a while."

Charesa took the fiddle and began to pluck the strings.

Frank began to do a Russian dance.

"Hey!" Frank said jumping up and down and putting up his arms like a Russian Cossack, "Hey! Hey! Hey!"

Charesa took the fiddle and began to bash it over and over again against the refrigerator door. Frank laughed and started to break dishes and turn over glasses of water.

"We're in Greece!" Charesa screamed and grabbed the kitchen towel and started to twirl it over her head. Frank locked arms, and they started to dance all over the apartment, kicking over furniture, and lamps and twirling dish towels.

The apartment was in shambles by the time the drink wore off, and Frank and Charesa collapsed, exhausted, on the living room floor.

After their laughter died down to a few chuckles here and there, Charesa suddenly jumped up, fixed her gown and sat down sedately on the couch like a queen.

"Lovely weather we're having today," she said in a haughty tone of voice.

Frank also jumped up suddenly and adjusted his tie. He put a pipe in his mouth and leaned against the wall with one hand in the pocket of his jacket.

"What did you say, dear?" he asked in a voice bearing a remarkable resemblance to a famous English actor.

"I said, lovely weather we're having," Charesa repeated.

"Yes, dear, I couldn't agree with you more," Frank responded and puffed on the pipe. The sweet aroma of the tobacco filled the room.

Outside, the weather was everything but delightful. The dark, ominous storm clouds had rolled right in over their city. Threatening thunder roared. Whips of lightning cracked out of the clouds every few seconds. The wind blew with the strength of a thousand soldiers, and the rain began to pour down like someone was pouring it from a bucket.

Frank drew the window curtains open, dimmed the lights, and put on some romantic music for the evening. He sat down on the couch beside Charesa and placed his arm ever so gently around her shoulder. The two lovebirds sat, watching the dazzling display of meteorological marvel, clutching each other desperately when the thunder and lightning hit a little too close to Frank's apartment.

"Oh Frank, oh Frank," Charesa said. "I do so want this evening never to end. It is so splendid. So delightful. So breathtakingly beautiful. Your whole house, your hospitality, your sense of humor, everything about you exudes the romance only love tales are made of. Oh, I feel so tired."

Frank leaned close to Charesa's ear.

"You wanna eat now?" he said.

Charesa didn't respond. She had fallen asleep and was snoring loudly. Frank clapped his hands. This was the moment he had been waiting for. He took her long, black hair in his hands and gently caressed it.

Within five minutes, it was all over!

Charesa woke up to a grinning face.

"Did you have a nice rest?" he asked her.

Charesa sighed. It was the most beautiful rest ever. She looked lovingly into Frank's eyes.

"Remember that expensive comb set you always wanted?" he asked.

"Comb set?" Charesa said, and in a moment of recognition as well as sheer horror, Charesa stared at herself in the hall mirror. There, looking back at her, was a woman with very little hair, if any. Frank had lovingly cut her cascading hair with its rivers of curls and had sold it to buy her a really cheap comb set!

"I hope you love it," Frank said in a wise, almost magi-like way. "With the rest of the money, I also bought myself a gold pocket watch."

The End

FAMILY VACATION

Joe and Jill had scrimped and saved for this vacation, even putting their children in day care. Jill worked two jobs instead of staying home, loving her children, giving them a well-rounded education, and building character into their little hearts.

They had saved $50,000!

And then... and then... the day of the family vacation had arrived!

Jill went to the beauty shop to have a complete makeover before their flight to Paris while Joe went to the barber and the dentist—just in case he might have a cavity. And the kids—well, the kids were zombied out from spending all day, each and everyday, in the hated day care center so that they couldn't care less what transpired between the time of preparation and the trip itself.

Both Jill and Joe packed all night to get ready for their flight the next day. In the morning, they were totally exhausted, but Joe managed to get the kids to the day care so that Jill could sleep all day.

Later in the afternoon, Jill woke up to find Joe still not home from work. In fact, his car was not yet in the garage. She called the day care, but Joe wasn't there. She had to take her car and pick up the kids herself!

At five o'clock, to the fulfillment of her horrible, nightmarish fears, Joe still had not come home. They had 30 minutes to get to the airport, and it took at least an hour to get there!

Jill told the kids to go to bed and promptly fell down and cried, spoiling her makeover.

At seven o'clock, Joe came home. He had gone out to get some groceries—milk, eggs, and cheese. Jill wasn't too upset that he had gone out and bought perishable items, but she was on the verge when she saw the ultra luxury sedan in the garage!

"I think we should save for Rome instead," Joe said, eating some cheese.

Jill was completely beside herself. All their hopes and dreams were dashed to pieces on their shiny, linoleum kitchen floor. The years of working two jobs and putting her beloved children in the day care now seemed as worthless as yesterday's news. Paris was the only thing that was going to save their marriage, their children, and her very life! What could they do with an ultra luxury sedan, for goodness sake? In their neighborhood, the hubcaps would be gone in five minutes, the rest of the car in ten.

Joe finished his cheese and wiped his fingers daintily on a napkin.

"Get the kids and get in the car, dear," he smiled, "I've rearranged our flight to Paris. We are now going around the world!"

Jill could not believe her ears! Joe must have surely lost his mind. They couldn't possibly afford an ultra luxury sedan and a trip around the world.

"But... but... " she stammered, "Joe, how can we possibly afford all this? And where did you go? Why were you so late in getting back? We were frantic!"

Joe smiled knowingly and winked at his wife in a secretive sort of way.

"Remember that sweepstakes ticket that I bought... " he chuckled.

They had won the million dollar sweepstakes, Jill thought disbelievingly, her world whirling about her like the Turkish dervishes that she had only read about but had never seen. She threw her arms around her wonderful husband.

"... Well, I think I'm going to win it," Joe concluded. "This is it, honey, I can feel it. Stick with me, babe."

Jill suddenly began to stare and stare and stare.

"You... you... think... that... you ... may... have. ...won... it?" she said like a monotone computer, but Joe didn't hear her as he packed the kids into the car and started the engine of the new ultra luxury sedan.

"Hey Jill, see how it runs?" Joe called out. "Come on, or we will be late for our plane to Pittsburgh."

"Pittsburgh?" Jill said. When she walked outside, Joe and the kids were driving round and round the cul-de-sac in the ultra luxury sedan so many times that she felt if they were tigers, they would soon turn to butter.

Joe stopped and beckoned his lovely wife to get into the car, but every time she tried, he would move a little farther. She tried hard not to shout and give in to her fierce anger, but it was beginning to get the better of her.

Finally, Joe let Jill get into the car and drove off as fast as the speed limit allowed, which was only 25 m.p.h.

"Are your seat belts fastened?" he asked Jill and then immediately put on the brakes so that Jill fell forward and hit her chin on the dashboard.

"Need to wear your seat belt, honey," Joe laughed. "Oh, by the way, I picked you up a little something on the way to the ultra luxury sedan car shop. Hope you like it."

Jill was in a state of horrible disbelief. Her husband had flipped out on her. What could possibly happen next? Her first instinct was to bonk him on the head with a sledgehammer, but she thought that she had better humor him or he might drive the car off a cliff.

"Uh . . . what were you saying, dear?" Jill asked. "Something about a present for me?"

Joe handed her a small, red package. He had generously sprinkled it with his cologne.

Jill quickly opened it and gasped. Joe had bought her a diamond bracelet! Jill, being an ex-jeweler's daughter, rapidly recognized the diamonds as being of the highest quality. Her mind swiftly calculated the cost of the diamonds. They were more than $60,000!

"Oh, Joe," Jill said, humoring him, "why . . . they are beautiful. Why didn't you buy more?"

Joe looked sad at this remark.

"You aren't satisfied, are you?" Joe asked her.

"Why . . . why, no honey. Not at all. It's lovely," Jill said, looking for some way for her and the kids to escape.

"Oh, by the way, Jill," Joe said, "you remember that remark about not being sure about winning the lottery?"

"Uh, yes," Jill replied.

"I lied," Joe said.

Jill suddenly stopped feeling bad about the diamond bracelet and quickly put it on.

"OH, JOE, IT IS SO BEAUTIFUL! OH, THANK YOU. THANK YOU VERY MUCH!" Jill screamed out.

". . . I lied about the lottery ticket," Joe said. "I never bought one."

And with that remark, Joe stepped on the gas.

Jill stopped looking at her bracelet.

"Oh God," she prayed, "please let me out of this car. . . "

All of a sudden, Jill read the date on a passing billboard sign all lit up in neon. It read "April 1, 1991."

"Why . . . why . . . that's it," she thought to herself. "Joe is playing a remarkably good April Fool's joke on me. Why, that little scamp! Ha, ha, ha."

Jill laughed out loud.

"Oh, Joe, you are such a clown," Jill said.

Joe looked at her menacingly. For, little did Jill know, earlier that day Joe had been in a meeting with his boss and co-workers. Right during an important and critical presentation by his boss, Joe said:

"Why don't you shut up."

There was a stunned silence.

Joe's boss, who was taken aback by Joe's comment, suddenly realized that Joe was only kidding. Perhaps his speech was a little too tense for the rest of the employees, and Joe wanted to reduce the pressure by interjecting a little humor.

"Ha-ha," Joe's boss said. "You are such a kidder, Joe."

"Oh yeah," Joe said taking an ink well and splashing it all over his boss's $700 suit, "take this!"

Now, there was definitely stunned silence. Joe's boss was furious.

Joe then proceeded to turn over the conference table.

"You're fired!" Joe's boss screamed. "Get out of here this instant!"

Joe, who was a day away from being vested in the company's retirement plan and eligible for the generous savings plan where the company matched contributions dollar for dollar, suddenly had nothing to live for.

"Yes, ha-ha," Jill said chuckling, "you are such a clown!"

"I was fired today," Joe said in a somber tone, "because I first told the boss to shut up, then poured ink all over his expensive new suit, and then turned over the conference table."

Jill screamed with laughter as if she had never heard anything funnier and clutched her stomach.

"I then went out, bought a gun, and robbed the bank," Joe continued. "The FBI should be looking for me by now."

Jill pounded her hands on the dashboard with tears streaming down her face, red with laughter.

"I fully intend to shoot myself with this gun," Joe concluded, brandishing a shiny, new revolver.

Jill finally gained control of herself and wiped the tears from her face.

"Oh, Joe! How can you make up such an outlandish story and even use little Joey's water gun as a prop," she chuckled as she grabbed the gun out of Joe's hand.

The gun suddenly went off and hit an expensive crystal vase on the floorboard shattering it into a million pieces. Jill went into shock.

"My . . . my vase!" she cried. "The very one my grandmother willed me. Ruined!"

The smoking gun fell from Jill's hand onto the floor.

"April Fool's," Joe said laughing as Jill began to sob hysterically.

"You're right. This gun is only a stage prop with blanks. The vase was a cheap, exploding joke. You can easily put it all back together. Ha-ha."

Jill looked at her husband in disbelief. She didn't know whether to laugh or cry. Joe's April Fool's jokes were going too far.

"Let me and the children off at the corner," Jill said.

"But Jill," Joe said, "this was really all an April Fool's joke—except for the fact that I was fired."

"You were fired?" Jill said. "That is no April Fool's joke!"

"Put a lid on it, Jill," Joe proclaimed. "Are we going on this vacation or not?"

"Vacation?" Jill said. "To Pittsburgh?"

"I have a better idea," Joe said. "Let's drop the kids off at grandma's and go to Paris by ourselves."

"Why . . . why . . ." Jill said, "but Joe, darling, that is what we were intending to do all along."

"I knew that," Joe said. "I just wanted to see if you remembered our plans since you were acting so crazy."

"I was acting crazy?" Jill said.

Later that night, quite late at that, they dropped the kids off at grandmother's house and proceeded to the airport, but not before Jill and her mother had a little mother-to-daughter talk.

"What do you mean he used a stage prop gun to act as if he had destroyed the expensive crystal vase Grandma Jones willed to you?" she said incredulously. "What manner of joke is this? I don't care if it is April Fool's. My precious little daughter should not be kidded that way. I don't care if he is your husband or the man in the moon, if you catch my drift."

"Really mother, I'd rather handle this myself," Jill said.

"Handle it yourself?" she said. "Handle it yourself? Ha! You can't even take care of your kids, and you think that you can take care of this horrible joke? Ha! Ha! I laugh in your face! HA!"

"Oh mother," Jill said. "You have never thought of me as a good mother."

"You don't know the rest of it, kiddo," Jill's mom replied.

"Ever since you were a little baby, I knew you'd end up with a loser like Joe. I knew it!"

"Look mother, I don't wish to discuss this any further," Jill said.

"Oh yeah," her mother said. "Well, you can just watch your kids all by yourself from now on. I don't care if your vacation is ruined or not!"

"Oh boo hoo, boo hoo," Jill sobbed. "No one cares for me, not even my own mother. Oh boo hoo, boo hoo."

Jill's mother sat in her rocking chair, looking quite smug. She was glad to see that she had made her daughter cry.

"And what's more, you're ugly, too!" her mother replied, dealing out the deathblow.

Jill became hysterical and sobbed huge, great sobs.

At that moment, Joe decided it would be a good time to tell his wife the truth. He had taken another job offer that would pay three times what he had been making at the other job, but, since he wanted to collect unemployment during the transition period, he had to get himself fired. He was also feeling quite sorry about the gun incident and the fact that he had been so cruel to his wife. He didn't know what had gotten into him. Yet, knowing that Jill was a reasonable, gentle, understanding wife, Joe decided to go, apologize, and start the vacation all over again with loads and loads of love and communication.

A screaming, hysterical monster resembling his wife greeted Joe. She menacingly brandished a knife from the kitchen and hurled herself at him. Joe wrestled with this she-devil and grappled for the knife. From the corner of his eye, he caught a glimpse of his mother-in-law rocking back and forth in the rocking chair with a smug grin on her face.

"Help me," he gasped. "Don't just sit there like a fool! Can't you see that she's lost her mind?"

"Rock-a-bye baby on the treetop . . ." she sang softly, still rocking back and forth.

Joe finally managed to wrench the knife from his wife's hand and flung her against the wall. She hit her head and crumpled to the floor.

"I don't know what got into her," he gasped, "I'm calling the police."

Joe reached for the telephone and felt an icy, cold hand upon his shoulder. He turned to see the evil glint in his mother-in-law's eyes. Suddenly, an expensive vase came down on his head and he fell to the floor.

Joe quickly woke up from his nap in cold sweat.

He couldn't believe that dream was so horrible. Yet, once he realized that his wife and kids were all packed and ready to go to Paris the next day, he sighed.

"Boy," he said, "what a nightmare."

Jill greeted him with a big hug and kiss.

"Did you have a nice nap, dear?" she inquired. "I'm so excited about our trip to Paris!"

"Honey, you wouldn't believe the dream that I had," Joe exclaimed. "I dreamt that I lost my job and we were in debt up to our ears and you tried to kill me . . . "

"Tut, tut," Jill replied as she brushed the hair from his forehead. "It's probably all the stress from planning the trip and all."

"I guess so," Joe said with a shrug and went downstairs. "I even dreamt that I bought an ultra. . . "

The sight of an ultra luxury sedan in the driveway and Jill's mother rocking back and forth in the living room was too much for Joe. He fainted dead away to the floor.

"Oh dear," Jill said running down the stairs. "Mother, I told you your surprise visits always excite him so!"

The End

GOODBYE, ROBERT

"Robert, I have something to give you before you leave," my wife said.

"Really?" Robert said. "I think I am going to cry."

"Oh, it's nothing to cry about," my wife told him. "Just a little something I thought you needed before you left. Actually, it is more like something you can give to us."

"Anything!" Robert said. "Name it."

"Five hundred seventy-six dollars and eighty-five cents."

Robert's mouth opened wide.

"And this is the bill."

"Bill?"

"Yes, for all the good deeds I did for you."

There was deathly silence. Robert appeared to be in a state of shock, but he quickly composed himself and examined the bill. Finally, without saying anything, he quickly took an envelope out of a box of envelopes that we had sitting nearby, took some money out of his wallet, stuffed it into the envelope, licked it, sealed it, and handed it to my wife.

"I think I need to be going."

"You just got here," my wife said.

"No, I really must be going."

"Well, before you go, we baked you a cake, and we want you to take it with you," my wife said.

"Are you going to charge me for that as well?"

"Why, Robert, why would we charge you for a going away cake?" my wife said. Then, we walked him to the door where my wife put the huge cake in his arms so that he couldn't see where he was going and walked into the wall instead of the elevator and the cake went into his face.

"Good-bye," we said and shut the door.

A little while later, I asked my wife:

"How much did he give us?"

"I don't know. I never checked."

She took Robert's envelope, looked inside, and then looked up with a slight frown.

"What's wrong?"

"This is not real money."

"What?"

"It's play money."

"What?"

My wife suddenly looked rather depressed.

After a few minutes of silence, I suddenly piped in, "I am tired of you always being used. Did he give you his flight number and time of departure?"

"Yes."

"Tomorrow, Robert will have a little going away party at the airport—sans five hundred odd dollars!"

The next day—which was the most beautiful day in all of mankind's history—my wife and I arrived at the airport at precisely 6:00 a.m. I was ready to get into a fist fight, but my wife told me to relax and be diplomatic. However, much to our chagrin, we found that the plane Robert had taken was not the plane he had told us. In fact, the only flight to Greece had been a plane that had left late last night. The next one was not until late that evening. Robert had duped us!

My wife started to cry. My fists started to clench up.

"I think it is time we both took a little vacation. We have enough money, and I have enough vacation hours accrued at work so that we could be gone for several weeks."

"What do you mean? You mean you want to go to Greece?"

That afternoon, in a whirlwind of packing and then unpacking, crating and then uncrating, we packed our suitcases and went to the airport to purchase two tickets to Greece. By nightfall, we were aboard a plane, traveling First Class, and holding each other's hands as we watched the city grow smaller and smaller during every climb and turn of the plane.

"You know, I love you," I said to my wife as she held my hand. "Even if we don't get the money, we will always have these memories."

"Yes, I know!" she squeezed my hand a little tighter.

"I mean it."

"I know you do."

"Stewardess, is the birthday cake ready?"

My wife's eyes grew big.

"Cake?"

"Happy Birthday, honey!"

"Birthday? It is not my birthday."

The stewardess and everyone in First Class clapped and began to sing happy birthday.

"Get up and give a speech."

My wife looked at me rather angrily.

"It is not my birthday. What has gotten into you?"

"Fine," I said and then to the stewardess. "Take the cake away."

The stewardess nodded and wheeled the pastry cart away from us and on down the aisle.

"Well, I hope you are pleased with yourself."

There was icy silence for the rest of the trip. Finally, when the hills of Athens were seen, my wife perked up again and grabbed my arm.

"Oh, I am sorry. Forgive me. If you wanted to celebrate my birthday early, it should have been okay with me."

"I don't want to talk about it."

When the plane finally came to a stop, I got up and took my small duffel bag out of the overhead compartment.

"I'll meet you at the hotel."

"Meet me?"

I quickly ran down the aisle, struggling through the people getting off the plane and making sure that my wife would not be able to keep up, got on the first bus to the terminal, went through Customs, left the suitcases for my wife to pick up, hailed a cab, and was off to the hotel in less than twenty minutes.

After checking in, I quickly made a phone call.

"Hello," I said. "May I please speak to Robert Blanding?"

"Yes, it is I, old boy," Robert said. "So glad you made it. Welcome to Athens."

"Robert, you were such a scream the other night when you ran into the wall with the cake."

"Oh, yes, I do my best to please, you know. By the way, how in the earth did you ever convince your wife to make up that phony bill?"

My fists began to clench up.

"Oh, it wasn't too hard."

"Well, meet me at the Hotel Acropolis at six. I'll have everything ready."

"Thanks," I said and hung up the phone.

Right then, the door opened and my wife stood in the entrance not looking particularly pleased. Her hair was frazzled.

"Honey, I located Robert! He wants to meet us tonight at six."

My wife dropped the bags.

"You left me at the airport."

"Didn't you hear what I just said?"

"First, the birthday party and now this."

"We must have got separated. I looked all over for you. I am so glad you made it."

"Robert is making you crazy," she said.

"We'll go see him and get the money!"

My wife sat on the bed and looked out the window.

"I'm tired."

"We'll see Robert, get the money, and I will punch him in the nose."

"Call him up and tell him that you will punch him in the nose tomorrow."

"Look, we came all the way over here to get the money, and, by Jove, we are going to do just that!"

My wife reluctantly got up and opened up one of the suitcases. She took out a very wrinkled outfit and went into the bathroom. When she did this, I quickly wrote a note telling her to meet us at the Hotel Acropolis and left. I had told Robert that I wanted to take my wife on a vacation to Greece. Since he was already going to be there ahead of us, I had him reserve a dining room in one of the nicest restaurants in Athens. He would have been invited to eat with us, but he was such a selfish brute that he was going to be punched in the nose.

It didn't take long for the taxi to arrive at the Hotel Acropolis. I hurried into the hotel lobby to find Robert. He was sitting on a settee and arose when I entered.

"There you are. Where is your wife?"

"I left her back in the hotel. Give me the money now or I will punch you in the nose."

"Money?"

"For my wife's bill."

Robert started to laugh.

"Oh yeah, Five hundred seventy-six dollars and eighty-five cents. Sure thing, old boy, I have it right here in my pocket."

Suddenly, I held my fist up to his face.

"See this? This is no joke!"

"But . . . " Robert protested, ". . . but I don't have that type of money!"

"Then you will have this!" I said and punched him in the nose.

Right then, my wife walked into the hotel and saw Robert on the floor holding his nose.

"Honey!"

She came over to where I was standing and grabbed hold of my arm.

"You're crazy. Stop it! We don't need the money!"

She bent down to see if Robert was okay.

"Robert, I'm so sorry. Are you okay? That bill was my husband's idea. He's a loony."

"And, if you come around our house again, you will get this!" I held up my fist again.

"Enough! Let's get out of here," my wife said. "Good-bye, Robert."

"I know of a really nice restaurant not far from here," I told my wife while we were walking away, "Would you care for a most scrumptious dinner?"

"That would be lovely," my wife said.

Robert watched us walk out of the Hotel Acropolis without saying a word.

The End

CHARA, GIRL OF THE EIGHTIES AND INTO THE NINETIES!

There wasn't a day gone by that Frank didn't think of Chara. Chara Jones, the Va-Va-Voom girl of the eighties and into the nineties. The very girl who wore maxi's and tee shirts and had red lipstick and long, curly brown hair down to the middle of her back.

Frank, dressed in a blue suit, with his hair parted in the middle, blew a kiss to his girl as though she was standing next to him on the veranda instead of walking down the street below him that very moment.

The very street where the early spring cherry blossom smell was un-missed and wafted over every house. Frank lifted his nose and snorted in the thick pollen filled night air. At the same time, a twinkle in the sky caught his eye and he saw a white star in the sky that was hid and then revealed by each and every passing graying cloud clouds that looked like cotton candy stuffed into medicine jars.

"This is a sign!" He clapped his hands. "Chara is coming over tonight for dinner!"

The table was set as usual with fantastic flair. On a crisp, clean, white tablecloth, freshly starched and pressed, lay steak and potatoes.

"Mmm," Frank said.

Frank pictured Chara sitting and enjoying every ounce of the meal.

He suddenly began to sob.

The doorbell rang.

"No! She can't be here already!" He ran into his bedroom, slammed the door and fell on his plush, king-size bed. He started to breath heavy and then...then...he started to flap his arms in excitement—a very rare type of involuntary movement.

"Quack! Quack!"

Chara was not at all pleased that Frank was not coming to open the door. She knew the date was still on since she could smell the fabulous dinner from the veranda. She suddenly heard something in the house like a giant bird.

Chara rang the doorbell several times. When that didn't work, she began to knock on the door. When that didn't work, she kicked the door several times, breaking the heel of her shoe in the process.

"Rats, rats, double rats!" Chara examined her shoe.

It was obvious that Frank was not going to answer the door. Chara decided to climb up the trellis and get in through the veranda doors.

Frank stopped quacking and flapping his arms long enough to hear someone climbing up the trellis outside his bedroom veranda.

"No!" He quickly waddled into the bedroom closet. He grabbed a golf club to brace himself from hitting the sides of the closet. However, this involuntary flapping was not only making a lot of noise since he kept hitting the sides of the closet with the club but was also making him mighty hungry. If he only could get to the kitchen before Chara saw him. He dropped the golf club.

"Quack, quack, quack!" he screamed and rushed downstairs just as Chara made it up the trellis and climbed over the veranda railing.

"Frank, Frank. . . ?" Chara asked. Suddenly she smelled something that made her mouth water.

"Frank. . . Frank...Frankfurters. Mmmm."

Frank was almost into the kitchen when he heard Chara's ravenous voice. They weren't even married and already she was upstairs screaming for food.

"I don't like aggressive females."

Chara crept downstairs.

"I hope he serves duck," she said.

When she walked into the kitchen, Frank turned and his eyes popped out of his head. Chara was stunning.

"Quack, quack, quack."

"Frank, you were here all the time!" Chara exclaimed.

Frank couldn't think. She was so beautiful.

"Quack, quack, quack."

Suddenly, one of his flapping arms hit Chara in the head. She promptly fell to the floor without any invitation. Frank hovered her for a moment and tried to make sense of what had just happened. He tried to call out her name, but all he could say was: "QUACK!"

Chara was a hopeless romantic. Her entire life was spent worshipping the very ground Frank walked upon. Whatever Frank did was mighty fine. Nothing was ever wrong. Nothing.

Frank poured a bucket of ice water on top of Chara's head.

"Are you alright?" he said. His involuntary movements had ceased. He was really embarrassed.

"Chara, I am really sorry," Frank said.

Chara looked at Frank and wiggled her mouth as though it was a beak. She was a penguin. The icy water that drenched her clothes refreshed her entire body. Frank helped her to her feet and she hit her arms several times against her body.

"Why don't we go out on the veranda and have a bite to eat."

Chara managed to rock back and forth on her frozen legs to make some forward movement.

"Quack," Frank said. No, he couldn't believe it. The involuntary movements were beginning again. He started to jump up and down and flap his arms.

Chara walked forward and ran into a wall. She turned, walked a few more steps and hit another wall. She turned and walked a few more steps and hit another wall.

"Quack, quack, quack." Frank screamed jumping up and down.

And now let's change the scene for a moment:

The policeman down the street—the one that would park and sleep—was rudely awakened by one of Frank's neighbors who had heard very strange sounds. The policeman, Edward P., was almost ready to retire with honors. He wasn't about to go and investigate weird noises just because someone thought he should.

"I really heard strange noises."

"Why don't you go home."

"I'm going to take a shotgun with me, next time."

"Never take the law into your hands."

"You mean don't take a gun and shoot people"

"No," Eddie said. "You should always let the police shoot people. If you hear any noise in the future, even it sounds like a dog, please contact your local police."

"I will," the civilian said.

The officer turned to leave. When he had gone a few paces, the civilian screamed. The officer turned quickly, gun drawn.

"I heard someone walking away from my house!" the civilian shouted.

The officer looked around and realized that he and the civilian were the only ones there.

"I'm the one walking away from your house."

"Boy, are you smart!"

Ed thanked the man for his compliment and walked away again. As he approached his squad car, he heard another scream.

"Wolf!"

Ed looked around again.

"What wolf?"

"Just having a little fun." The neighbor who was also the civilian burst out laughing. He laughed so hard his body shook and his eyes bulged out. Ed turned away in disgust. Pulling away, he heard another scream:

"Wolf, wolf, wolf. . . ah…"

And now back to the Frank and Chara Show:

Frank had already knocked over the table. The steak and potatoes were strewn all over the veranda. Chara was sitting on her chair rocking back and forth.

Frank tried to say: "Would you care for more wine?" but all he could say was: "Put in on my bill."

Chara got up from her seat and waddled over to the edge of the veranda where she promptly fell to the street below. Frank's eyes grew as big as saucers. His date was ruined. His involuntary movements and Chara's equally weird behavior was responsible for this evening's fiasco.

Suddenly, a police car, careening carelessly out of control, came down the street straight at Chara's limp body on the sidewalk. Frank knowing that he needed to run down, pick up Chara's body, and drag it to safety before the car slammed into her, started to excitedly jump up and down and flap his arms even more. It was a horrible date.

Conclusion:

When a police car, or any other moving vehicle for that matter, is driven by a wolf, the said vehicle will be unable to slow down or even stop because the wolf's paw is not physically able to reach the brake pedal. However, there is a chance that a very clever wolf could stop the vehicle if it was a handicap vehicle specially designed with hand levers. Fortunately for Frank and especially for Chara, the police car was one such vehicle and the wolf was incredibly clever. Hence, the car came to a screeching halt within inches of Chara's limp body.

Frank couldn't wait to express his gratitude to the driver of the car.

"I'll be right down."

Frank ran downstairs and outside. While he did this, Chara lifted her head weakly.

"Frank, " she said in a whisper.

"You ruined our date," Frank said and quickly opened the door of the police car.

"Grrrrrr."

"Uh. . . " Frank said. "Nice doggie."

"Quick, there are some dog biscuits in the front seat!" It was Ed speaking from the back seat.

"Oh there you are," Frank said. "I just want to say. . . "

The wolf was not very pleased with the ensuing conversation and lunged for Frank's throat.

Conclusion continued:

Chara slowly took hold of the trellis and pulled her badly bruised body up to the veranda. She stiffly sat down looking at the over turned table. Perhaps she could salvage what was left of the evening. She bent down and picked up a cracked champagne glass. She looked up into the evening sky. The clouds were beautiful. The cherry blossoms smelled great. The sound of a summer sprinkler on a newly cut lawn was symphonic.

"Frank? Frank? Where are you Frank?"

"Chara…Chara…quack…QUAAAAAKKK…Aaahhhh!"

The End

THE MAGIC SHOW

Frank told Chara to close her eyes, and he would give her a big surprise. Chara complied, puckering her lips, drawing closer to her love. Suddenly, her lips caressed a piece of cardboard.

"Surprise!" Frank told Chara. "Two tickets to San Juan, the Cuban Magician and his magic pony! I camped out all night long to get tickets. These were a steal at $50 dollars apiece! Normally they are $1.25 each, but this time I had to buy them from a scalper."

The next day, Chara, in an expensive evening gown and a diamond tiara on her head, and Frank, in a rented tuxedo, sat, the only two people in a desperately vacant theater, for the opening of the San Juan Magic Show.

San Juan was dressed in elegant garb. He wore an Indian turban almost half the size of his body on his head.

"Sorry, but the magic pony is sick today. Let's get to know each other a little better. What's your name, folks?"

"This is my lovely fiancée, Chara!" Frank said clapping.

San Juan suddenly picked up a grapefruit and threw it straight at Chara. The grapefruit hit her in her face, splattered, and some of the splatter knocked the tiara off into the back row.

Frank didn't clap.

"What's your name, son?" San Juan said.

"Frank Jones."

"Well then, Frank, have a 'welcome' grapefruit, too!" He threw a grapefruit at Frank with great vigor. The grapefruit caught Frank in the stomach and threw him over three seats.

Chara, coming to, weakly put her hand to her head.

"Where. . . where is my tiara?" she said.

"Here's a fruit tiara!" San Juan threw another grapefruit hitting Chara straight between the eyes.

"This is an outrage!" Frank screamed, rising to his feet.

"Oh, you don't like my magic tricks?"

"Magic tricks? All you are doing is throwing grapefruit at us!"

"Them's fighting words, mister." San Juan took out five huge, delicious grapefruits from a trunk on the stage. "I think you need a lesson in what magic is all about!"

San Juan began to pelt Frank with the grapefruit.

"Here's a lesson, and there's a lesson, and here's another lesson!"

"I. . . I. . . can't believe this is happening!" Frank said. "C'mon Chara. Let's get out of here!"

A grapefruit whizzed past their heads.

Chara weakly sat up taking Frank's hand. At that very moment, a grapefruit hit Frank, knocking him on his knees.

"You know, you are really a beautiful woman," Frank said to Chara. "Will you marry me?"

Chara quickly ducked when she saw another grapefruit and came close to Frank's face.

"Oh, Frank," she said.

"Oh, Chara."

Another grapefruit hit Frank's head in such a manner that he lurched forward and planted his lips onto Chara's.

"What a magical evening this is, folks. The two lovebirds have proposed." San Juan said and picked up two "wedding" grapefruits.

"These are on the house!" He lunged two more ripe grapefruits right square dab on Chara and Frank's head.

And now, this is where this story begins to wax philosophic. Love conquers all. And for all the grapefruits and magician joints in the world, nothing could keep these young people from loving each other with a pure, deep love, even if they were covered with grapefruit pulp. So, on a fine summer evening, with a beautiful breeze and crickets happily chirping, with the sound of children laughing and playing ball in the streets, with the distant hum of a lawn mower finishing the day's chores so that someone could sit drinking lemonade and rejoice at the missing grass, Frank and Chara promised each other faithfulness for the rest of their natural lives.

And what about our matchmaker, San Juan? Well, he would go on with his magic shows, throwing grapefruits at the audience, and remembering the magic he had helped to bring about in this one couple, the joy that he had brought to them by the one solitary good deed that he had ever accomplished in his miserable, wasted life.

And that is about it.

The End

MRS. MONKEY

"Gather around, ladies and gentlemen, and watch how easy it is to make Mrs. Monkey mad," the barker said.

Mrs. Monkey sat still, passive, with a gentle and quiet spirit. The sun was shining and a little breeze was blowing through her cage.

The barker took a grocery receipt and showed Mrs. Monkey that she had been overcharged by $7.51.

When Mrs. Monkey found out she was not going to be reimbursed, she immediately jumped up and down and screeched to high heaven.

"She'll do that all day, folks," the barker said, ". . . and all for $7.51!"

The next day, the barker showed a calm and contented Mrs. Monkey an unneeded bottle of blue cheese salad dressing that had been purchased for $0.86.

Immediately, Mrs. Monkey started to jump up and down again howling and showing her teeth. She took hold of the bars of her cage and shook and rattled them.

"All for eighty-six cents, folks. . . all for eighty-six cents!" the barker said to a capacity crowd.

Mrs. Monkey was the hit of the circus.

The End

THE GROOVY DATE

George was hopelessly in love with Irene. She was everything he had ever wanted. Tonight would be a special night for George had been invited over to Irene's for dinner—for the very first time! The dinner date was set for seven o'clock, and Irene had told him not to be late as she would have prepared a scrumptious dinner for the two of them.

George adjusted his tie and knocked on the door. The vision of beauty that greeted him nearly took his breath away. Irene stood there in the doorway, dressed in a stunning red evening gown. Behind her, soft music was playing. George walked in and beheld a beautiful table set for two on the veranda. Irene had used her best china and silverware. Crystal champagne glasses glimmered in the moonlight and soft candles cast a romantic glow over the whole table.

George was over two hours late.

He was dressed in a green seersucker suit with a bright red tie and an orange shirt.

Irene was still standing at the doorway with her mouth wide open while George wandered through the various rooms in Irene's penthouse. She finally recovered enough to shut the front door and turn to George. Just looking at him hurt her eyes. He looked like a Christmas elf!

"I brought you a present," George said, handing Irene a bunch of ragweed he had picked out of the vacant lot across the street.

George then walked over to the elegantly spread table and picked up a crystal champagne glass.

"Expensive?" he asked Irene.

"What . . . you bought it for me . . . don't you remember?" Irene asked.

"Yeah . . . " George said, "I forgot. Hey, you wanna see something funny?"

Suddenly, a squirt of black ink came out of a fake flag on his lapel.

Irene quickly grabbed a napkin from the table and wiped her face. She rubbed black ink all over her face.

"Eeee-eeee, help me! Help me!" Irene said and furiously rubbed her face to get the ink off.

"I'm blind! I can't see! Eeeeeeeee."

Oh, my poor readers, right then Irene began to sneeze. And sneeze. And sneeze. AND SNEEZE! You're right! She was allergic to ragweed and George was holding the bouquet right under her nose, waiting for her to notice them.

"Get . . . those . . . things . . . out . . . of . . . my . . . face," Irene sputtered between sneezes. "Ah-choo! Ah-choo! Aaaaaah-chooooooo!"

George quickly ran over to the kitchen, found the delicious pie that Irene had spent hours preparing from scratch, grabbed it, and threw it in Irene's face.

"Merry Christmas!" George said.

Irene stumbled around the room looking for something, much like a blind hog. She finally found a delicious Boston Chocolate Cream Pie and threw it full force at George. But, alas, he caught her hand and directed her hand right into her own face. Splat! Boston Chocolate Cream Pie all over her face and dress.

"My Boston Chocolate Cream Pie!" Irene screamed.

"Hey! Watch this!" George said. He ran to the table and pulled the tablecloth with everything on it to the floor.

"Tah-dah!" he screamed. "Presto! Now you'll never need to clean again!"

Irene screamed in frustration and tried to jump on George. She wanted nothing better than to punch his grinning face, but she missed him and fell on the floor instead. With the floor so slippery from a fine afternoon waxing, Irene slid headfirst into the wall headfirst!

"Grrrrr . . . grrrrr," Irene said.

Uh . . . my dear readers . . . did I forget to mention that Irene was a mental patient. Uh. . . let me clarify, please. . . she had been a mental patient. Yes, Irene had just gotten out of intensive and extensive psychiatric care. She had done so well over the past five years that the doctors had finally decided that she was well enough to be released with only periodic follow-ups. When she saw George after all these years in the nut house, she couldn't remember anything but the fact that there was something about the past with George that was all too real. Of course, she had reasoned, it had to be love. Only love! But it wasn't love! No. It wasn't love. It was madness! Georgie Porgie had driven her to the funny farm.

George couldn't believe what was happening. He had come to cheer Irene up, not drive her mad again. He really loved her. Loved her with all his heart and was only being funny. But now, Irene was acting really strange and wasn't laughing either. In fact, she was growling like a bear. Like a big old grizzly.

"Irene! Irene?" George said tenderly bending down and touching her lips. "Are you well, my sweet?"

No, Irene was not well. She was a grizzly now and there was nothing you could do about it.

George quickly ran to get the police, but then something funny happened. Ha. Ha. George slipped on the banana soufflé that Irene had made out of love and slid right into the wall.

When George came to, all he could do was hold his hands up and say:

"Grrr-grrrrr. I am a grizzly bear."

"And I am a grizzly bear, too!" Irene said and held her hands up even higher than George's to show how ferocious she was.

And that, my dear readers, is how George and Irene became a couple of old grizzly bears.

The End

THE OFFICE BARTER SYSTEM

At my office, we have an interesting system. If you bring a peanut butter sandwich and someone comes by your desk and sees it and wants it, it is okay for that person to take it as long as he replaces it with an equivalent form of food. For instance, if you have a box that has six chocolate mints on your desk, the acceptable form of exchange is two tangerines. If you have an apple, then a peanut butter sandwich is acceptable.

This went well for awhile. Everyone was quite happy, and it seemed that no one was ever disappointed as the equitable form of exchanges was consistent. But, as normally happens in this kind of system, something breaks down, and, when this happens, everyone gets confused and is hesitant to exchange anything for fear of offending someone in the office.

The reason for the breakdown was this—someone had exchanged a pear for two apples. Now, in the Office Barter System, fruits are considered fair exchanges. One banana for one apple. One orange for one banana. You see what I am saying. But this time, someone bypassed the fair and equitable exchange and stole one apple.

And now, this is where it really broke down! I came back from a meeting and there, sitting beside my desk, was a stack of watermelons. I am not talking about one or two watermelons. I am talking about twenty or so. I thought to myself, what in the world did I have on my desk to exchange for twenty watermelons? And that is when I noticed that my computer had been taken!

"Alright?" I said, quite mad. "Who took my computer?"

But no one answered since they were all at an important meeting.

"Well, two can play at this game!" I said and took all the watermelons and put them in my boss's office and grabbed his chair and his winter coat.

When my co-workers got back from the meeting, they were, of course, surprised to hear our boss scream. Of course, my boss wasn't the only one screaming, for when Joe opened his desk drawer looking for a pen, there was none to be found. Instead, he had six chocolate mints.

"What is going on here?" my boss said, coming out of the office and looking suspiciously at everyone looking suspiciously at him. "Who stole my chair and my winter coat?"

"Who stole my pens?" Joe demanded.

"Who stole my rutabaga pie?" Sally said and held up, instead of the pie, one large french fry with a dab of ketchup on the end.

I had, of course, anticipated this. And, not to lay the blame on me, I had quickly disassembled the chair and had hidden it in my desk along with the winter coat, various pens and rutabaga pie.

"Who took my computer?" I also demanded.

Everyone looked at me.

"My computer is missing as well," I said.

My boss stared at me for the longest time, such that I started to feel guilty from his hard stare.

"Your computer?" he said. "Didn't you take your computer down to the service shop this morning?"

With a sudden brilliant memory of that very morning, I remembered everything I had done. Yes, I had taken my computer down to be repaired. Yes, it had a problem with its disk drive and needed to be thoroughly cleaned in order to insert and eject a disk.

"And I thought someone had exchanged all those water . . ." I said and then suddenly stopped.

"All those what?" my boss demanded. "All those watermelons? All those watermelons I gave to each and everyone one of you from the produce of my watermelon farm?"

It was then I noticed, and I don't know how I could have missed it, that in each of my co-workers' cribs was a stack of twenty or more watermelons.

"You have my chair and my winter coat, don't you?" my boss said.

"And my pens."

"And my rutabaga pie!"

"Yeah!" I said. "And I have something else, too!"

And with that, I held up my pink slip for everyone to see. And after they had seen it, I packed everything up and went home.

And that is how I became a writer.

The End

WORLD COURT

The Indians were fit to be tied. They had their day in court, but it was night before they were finished. The dawn of a new day would not shine on their sullen faces or bring rays of hope to their broken dreams. The World Court had spoken. So be it. There would be no money for the white man taking their land. Justice was not retroactive beyond a period of 200 years said the Court. This went for all historical events, not limited to just the Indians. The dignified, stoic faces masked the anger the Indians felt toward such a decision. Justice was blind. It shouldn't be limited to just injustices committed in the past 200 years. But the World Court would hear of no further nonsense. Case closed. Then it happened. Just when the Indians and the rest of the tribes of the nations of the worlds had finally accepted the fact, the past reared its ugly head again and no one could do anything about it. For it had happened 250 years ago, and the World Court's decision was final. There was no undoing what the World Court had decreed. Even the World Court had to abide by its interpretation. There was absolutely nothing it could do. Absolutely nothing!

Let there be no mistake about this. When people saw him, they knew him. They didn't understand how he had not aged for 250 years, but it was him all the same. The same walk. The same way he parted his hair. The same small black mustache. The same insignia on his sleeve.

Even though he removed the insignia, donned regular clothes, and became a gardener outside of Bremerhaven Shipping Yard, the response of the people was all the same:

"You killed others! Kill yourself!"

And this is where it gets complicated. For the law explicitly outlawed prejudices centuries earlier with an emphasis on forgiveness. All those not forgiving and forgetting were fined 50,000,000 marks. And soon all those in Bremerhaven were receiving stern warnings from the World Court warning them that if they did not want to spend the rest of their lives as paupers, they had better get on with the task of forgiveness. But the people did not care a smidgen for what the World Court said and desired nothing more than this swine to be thrown back into the hole he had crawled out of.

Of course, the Indians were quite eager to see whether the World Court would follow through with its threats, for if it didn't, they were going to really raise a stink and sue the USA for every penny it owned! And the World Court said:

"No Way!"

So, the next day, the fine people of Bremerhaven were all given notice that they would be fined 50,000,000 marks apiece.

"Fine," the people all said. "If the World Court wants it, let them enforce it!"

And no one in Bremerhaven dared raise their hand against their brother since they were all united in their animosity toward this dark figure of world history. The World Court was outraged.

"How dare! How dare they! They will all likewise perish!"

And here, history had a strange turn of events. For the World Court finally came to the conclusion that sometimes the need for genocide is imperative for the good of the rest of mankind. And so, the World Court passed a law that whoever would not pay the fine would be instantly incinerated. And the people of Bremerhaven didn't care so the entire city of Bremerhaven was nuked.

Of course, the gardener died in the blazing inferno, but the World Court didn't care about this either. For sometimes, justice is better served when one man dies among the many, than for the many to live and kill the one man.

Or something like that.

The End

MY FIRST ALIEN ENCOUNTER

Now, I must say at the beginning, I do not believe in alien encounters. This is just my belief. UFO spottings are either devils in disguise or angels or swamp gas or some other logical explanation, but nothing as wonderful as man created in the image of God. This disbelief also extends to believing that amoebas swimming around some type of primeval planetary stew or carbon-based life forms burrowing around some rock suddenly decide to get up and reside in some God forsaken place like Antarctica!

Now, I must have rolled my eyes a dozen times before Robert came to the conclusion that I was an infidel and stopped telling me about all the alien encounters that seemingly intelligent people purported to have had. He really didn't know how to approach me, but he did manage to spit out:

"I would think that as an engineer you would believe."

"Listen, Robert. I bet you that if we went and visited one of these people who have claimed to have witnessed a sighting, you would come away just as skeptical as I am."

"Put your money where your mouth is," Robert Smith, Ph.D., said.

"Where is that book you have on extraterrestrial phenomena?" I asked.

Robert reached into his coat pocket and pulled out a yellow, tattered book. He handed it to me. I flipped the book open to sightings in our city and fell on a page with a picture of a young woman who had been abducted by some sort of alien.

"Let's go visit this girl," I said.

Robert agreed and we put on our coats and got in the car.

Soon, we were on the street where she lived. We found her house and stopped the car. Robert quickly got out of the car and headed for the house. I got out and followed. When we got to the door, we didn't have to knock or ring the doorbell because it suddenly swung open to reveal an old, gray-haired lady missing several teeth.

"Visitors!" she said.

"Hello, I am Dr. Robert Smith," Robert said, "and this is Mike, one of my friends. I am sorry to bother you, but we are looking for a Miss Alveris who is shown in this book."

Robert held the book up for the lady to see. She looked at the picture and started to laugh.

"What they won't do to sell a book!" she said.

Robert and I didn't know what to say.

"I'm Miss Alveris," the lady said to our shock.

"But the lady in the picture is so young," Dr. Smith said.

"Yes! That is why I laughed."

"You were abducted by aliens?"

Miss Alveris started to laugh again and hold her sides.

"Oh, what they won't do to sell people books!"

"Miss Alveris, this book says that you said you were abducted by aliens," Robert said.

"And you believed that?"

I looked to Robert and smiled, but he didn't acknowledge it.

"Sorry to have bothered you, ma'am,"

When we were back in the car, Robert confided in me.

"I think Miss Alveris was abducted and this woman was substituted in her place."

"Oh c'mon," I said.

"No, really. You gotta believe me. I really think that Miss Alveris was kidnapped, and this is an alien who is here to spy on earth," Robert said.

I looked briefly back at the house. Suddenly, something, I don't know what it was, something green, flashed by the front window. I thought maybe the sun was playing tricks with my eyes, but I saw something all the same. And it didn't seem normal.

"Robert," I said, "let's go and have some lunch. I think I need something to eat. My mind is playing tricks on me."

Robert was startled at what I just said.

"What's the matter?"

"Nothing, but I thought I saw something mighty odd suddenly flash by Miss Alveris's living room window."

"Like what?"

"Like a green flash of something that was too 'unsomething' to be really something," I said, wondering what I was saying.

Robert started the car, and we went down to the local burger place. I had a nice big cheeseburger with fries and a soda. Robert had a fish sandwich and an orange soda. The sauce on the fish sandwich was delicious. I put a little more salt on my burger because it wasn't that salty, but the fries were okay. The ketchup in this burger joint was really good, and I dipped my burger into it.

"I'm glad you said let's do lunch," Robert said. "I didn't know how hungry I was!"

After eating, we drove back to Miss Alveris's house. When we got there, we both looked at each other for the type of explanation we were going to use to go back to see her.

"I know," I said. "Let's say that we want her to autograph your book."

Robert thought that was a brilliant suggestion and hurriedly got out of the car. I once again got out and followed.

We rang the doorbell. In a few minutes the door opened and, to our surprise, there was a young lady. In fact, it was the same lady in the book.

"May we speak to Miss Alveris, please?" Robert asked.

"Yes? May I help you?" the lady answered.

"You are Miss Alveris?"

"Yes," the lady said and suddenly she saw the book that Robert was holding.

"Oh no! Not again! Are you here to ask me about my alien abduction?"

"Well . . ."

Suddenly, the lady began to cry.

"It was terrible. I don't know how to explain it. I don't believe in aliens, but there they were! Oh . . . it was horrible."

Robert and I stood not knowing what to do next. Quickly, I took Robert's book and held it up to the lady.

"Would you mind signing this? We really would like your autograph."

The woman looked up and tried her best to compose herself. "Do you have a pen?"

Robert handed her a pen, and the real Miss Alveris signed her name the best she could do while she was sobbing.

Robert took the pen and the book back and thanked her for her autograph. He turned to me, and I nodded that we needed to be going.

"Sorry to have disturbed you," Robert said. "We will not bother you again."

"It's okay," she said and then went back to crying. After she shut the door, we both walked back to the car in silence.

We got in and drove back to work.

"Well," I said, "maybe there is some truth here."

After we drove away, the young lady stopped crying and started laughing. An old lady walked out of the back bedroom wearing a bright green rubberized alien monster suit. She took off the mask and began to laugh.

"The things we do to sell our books!" she said, and the two women fell on each other, laughing with glee.

The End

A FUND EXPERIMENT

"Now," Robert told his wife, "I am going on a long trip. You won't see me for years, but I will come back and see you."

"Where are you going?"

"I am going into the future. I am sure you will be angry when you see me, but it won't be for long, because once I have seen you, I will vanish again and you will see me standing in this very spot exactly five minutes from now."

Robert's wife was puzzled.

"I am curious about what our 401k will do if I invest in certain options and leave them," he said. "I've decided to go twenty years into the future and see the outcome."

"What if you can't come back?"

A slight pause—then, "I hope I made the right choice."

"What do you want for dinner?"

"I wouldn't make anything for me now, but, five minutes later, I will tell you what I want."

Robert left for the basement. His wife, still confused but knowing that Robert was a puzzling man, went to the kitchen to make dinner, with or without her husband's request.

She was quite unsure what to make of it all, but, after a few minutes, she quickly forgot the conversation.

Later in the afternoon, Robert's wife walked over to the basement door and knocked. She waited. She knocked again, and again nothing. Finally, she opened the door and walked down to the basement. Robert was nowhere to be seen. She hadn't heard him come up. Where had he gone?

When supper was ready and the light outside had turned a dim color, Robert's wife called out his name, but no one answered. The house was quite still.

"I don't like this," she thought. "He's never been late for dinner before."

Robert's dinner grew cold, and his wife placed it in the oven to keep warm hoping he would notice it when he came back. In the morning, Robert's plate was still warm in the oven. He had never touched it. His wife looked for him again and called out his name, but it was to no avail—he wasn't in the house.

After several days, Robert's wife contacted the authorities and told them what had happened. They searched the house for clues, but all they could find was a slightly discolored spot on the basement floor.

"Did he say anything before he left?" they asked.

"I'll be back in five minutes," she said.

After the authorities had left, and after several more days, weeks and months, the case was officially closed. Robert was missing, but since no foul play could be determined, it was decided that he had just deserted his wife. Robert's wife was not pleased.

Years passed, and Robert's wife was able to secure a job that kept her living slightly above poverty level. Day after day, while working, she cursed her husband for leaving her. She would never forgive him. Never! Her face became more wrinkled, and the pretty smile she once wore turned into a permanent scowl.

Finally, twenty years to the day her husband had left, Robert's wife was sitting at the kitchen table when she heard a noise coming from the basement. She immediately got up in fright. Who was down there? She heard footsteps slowly walking up the stairs, and—finally—the door flew open and there, before her eyes, was none other than Robert. He didn't look any different from when he had left.

"You!" she managed to say.

"Okay, what's the value of our 401K?" Robert asked.

"Where have you been?"

"That doesn't matter. What matters is the value of our 401K. I need to know whether I invested wisely or not."

"You left me twenty years ago with nothing to live on and expect to find anything left of the 401k?"

"You spent it all?" Robert asked. "Oh great . . . that's just great. I'll be right back."

Robert turned and went down into the basement.

"Robert? Robert, where are you…" Robert's wife said but suddenly saw a brilliant blue flash of light and then nothing. Robert had vanished again.

Robert's wife went back to the kitchen table. She sat down and tried to think of what had happened. Her mind was muddled. She couldn't think. The 401k had been…had been…she thought…left untouched when Robert had first left, but now…she was beginning to remember different things. The 401k had been placed in a trust. A trust where she couldn't touch the money for twenty years. Then, she remembered that when the authorities had informed her that Robert had deserted her and was never located, that she had him declared legally dead so the trust would be legally hers without waiting for twenty years.

Another flash of light in the basement, more footsteps, and Robert walked into the kitchen.

"The value?"

"I told you I spent it."

"I put it in a trust."

"I had you declared legally dead." Robert's wife said.

"Oh bother," Robert said. "I'll be back."

A flash of light and Robert's wife was again confused.

"Did I say spent it? Spent what?" she thought. She had tried to obtain some money after Robert had left her. When she had gone to inquire how much was in their 401k, she had found out that Robert had withdrawn the money and had hidden it somewhere—but where?

Another light and Robert was there in the kitchen again.

"Do you know what you put me through? You left me nothing to live on."

"This will all be a bad dream," Robert said.

"If it wasn't for some gold coins that I found buried in the backyard, I would never have survived."

"You found the gold coins?"

"So that's where you hid the money!" Robert's wife said. "Good. I'm glad I found it and spent it all!"

Robert went back into the basement and disappeared. His wife sat still for awhile, expecting him to reappear, but he never did. She got up and went to cook. She thought of her husband and tried to remain bitter against him. She suddenly couldn't think of what would make her bitter. Deserted her? He had never deserted. What an imagination she must have. As she opened a cupboard, Robert walked into the kitchen.

"Have you decided what you want for dinner?" she asked. "I haven't started making anything yet."

"Leave me alone, I'm not hungry," Robert said and sat down at the kitchen table.

"What's wrong?"

"Can't you keep your grubby hands off our money for at least twenty years?"

"What?"

"I can't leave you for a measly twenty years without you spending every dime we have!"

"What are you talking about, honey? You've only been gone for five minutes. Anyway, if you really did leave me for twenty years, you better leave me something to live on!"

Robert looked at his wife and suddenly smiled. He picked up the phone and called their insurance agent.

"I think I want steak for dinner," he said, ". . . and lobster!"

The End

HAPPY CHINESE NEW YEAR!

"Happy New Year!" Mike said, but Jerry didn't care since New Year for him was January 1st and not February 8th like in this country.

"What are we going to give the guards?" Mike said since it was customary to give the local workers a gift at this time of the year. "Whiskey?"

Jerry looked up at him in disgust.

"Haven't you heard of the Foreign Corrupt Practices Act?" he said. "Fifty dollars! That's all we are going to spend on gifts!"

"Okay. You know, we could buy twelve cases of soda. A case for each guard might be nice. Their family would appreciate it."

"I have already decided what to give them," Jerry said. "Go down to the key store and have them make up twelve key chains with our company logo on them."

Mike wanted to remind Jerry that the guards were poor and would not appreciate such a measly gift, but he knew from experience that it was useless trying to reason with him. He took the $50 from Jerry and went out to his appointed task.

A few hours later, he came back with the key chains in a small brown paper sack. He handed Jerry the change—$48.50. Jerry told Mike to leave early and give the key chains to the guards.

"I thought, since you are the manager, that you might want to give them the key chains."

"What do I have in common with Chinese New Year?" Jerry said. "Now go and do what I tell you!"

Mike reluctantly went out of the office. When he got into his car and drove to the main gate, he noticed that there were several cars ahead of him that were stopping and giving the guards New

Year gifts. He watched as they handed them crates of oranges, huge gift boxes of cooking oil (very expensive in this country) and traditional cookies. Mike was glad that the custom was not to open the gift in front of you. He drove up, rolled down the window, and gave the main guard the small brown paper bag. After wishing them a prosperous New Year, he drove off as quickly as he could.

"I have never been so embarrassed in all my life."

The next day, the guards met Mike at the gate and informed him that from then on, all subcontractors had to park in the remote parking lot, which was a mile down the road. Mike drove to the lot and parked his car. Jerry was waiting for him.

"What did you do yesterday to get the guards mad at us?"

"I didn't do anything but give them the key chains," Mike said. "They probably were insulted by the stupid, cheap gift."

"No! You did something! I know it!" Jerry said, and both men walked in silence to their office.

For the next year, Mike and Jerry's relationship deteriorated. Jerry barely spoke with Mike except to ask for specific tasks. His face stayed red most of the time and steam came out of his ears and nostrils. When Chinese New Year arrived again, Mike decided to make amends.

"I am going to give the guards a good gift this year," Mike said, "then we will be able to park near our building."

Jerry was fit to be tied. It wasn't the gift; it was something Mike had done.

"You get them a set of back scratchers. They cost about two dollars each. Here is twenty-four dollars."

Mike couldn't believe it. This would never do. Jerry just refused to open his eyes and realize what he was doing. This was not America; this was a foreign country.

"Okay," Mike said and took the twenty-four dollars. However, Mike didn't go and buy back scratchers. Instead, he waited until he saw Jerry leave for home and took all the money out of the petty cash fund.

"We'll get our parking lot back or my name isn't Mike," Mike said and went out and bought, not back scratchers, but 1200 key chains with the company logo. "One key chain is a cheap gift. One hundred is more like it."

Mike put all the key chains in a huge garbage bag and dropped them off at the main gate.

"Happy New Year!" Mike drove off, happy and content that the next day he and Jerry would be able to park in the main plant once again.

The next day, the guards stopped Mike and told him that the remote parking lot was closed to the likes of him and his squirrelly boss. From then on, they must park in the remote, remote parking lot. Mike's face fell. This was tragic. How was he ever going to face Jerry?

His hands shook as he drove out of the main plant and to the remote, remote parking lot.

When he passed by the remote parking lot, he noticed that it was chained off with what looked like multiple key chains. When he got to the remote, remote parking, he saw Jerry looked redder than ever and had what looked like a pitchfork in his hand.

"Hi Jerry, how's it going?" Mike said and waved as he drove into the parking lot. Jerry didn't say anything but made loud "TOOT! TOOT!" noises and brandished his pitchfork.

"Now, I know what you are going to say," Mike said, getting out his car.

"TOOT!"

"I tried to appease the guards. I guess they wanted more than one hundred key chains a piece."

"TOOT! TOOT!"

"I was going to get them back scratchers, but I decided they could always pick up a stick and use it as a back scratcher. The next obvious choice was a gift of multiple key chains with, of course, our company logo strategically and predominately displayed."

"SPUTTER! SPAT! TOOT!"

Mike decided he had better start walking to work. It was ten miles away, but he knew that if he walked fast, he should be able to get there by break time. He looked back to see if Jerry was going to follow him, but Jerry was still hissing and snorting and blowing steam.

"He'll get over it," Mike thought. "He just needs to learn how to live with this culture."

"Have a little humor!" Mike yelled back at Jerry and then to himself: "Yeah, that's it. Have a little humor. Can't survive overseas long without humor."

As Mike continued walking, he could hear Jerry laughing. He could also hear breaking glass and tires being deflated, and Jerry still laughing to beat the band.

"I'm glad he's beginning to liven up. I think this is going to be a good year," Mike said. "Yes, Happy Chinese New Year!"

The End

FRED'S PSYCHO WIFE'S LUNCHEON

Now this is what happened—

It innocently started out as an invite to lunch for all the workers in the office. Our boss's new wife was a gourmet cook, and we wanted to taste her cuisine. I couldn't tell you how much we enjoyed it. The food was so delicious that his wife could have died, and no one would have noticed.

This luncheon idea caught on with the rest of the wives who lived overseas and had nothing better to do but play bridge. Soon, they were all trying to outdo one another.

"Please remember my wife is on the verge of a nervous breakdown," Fred said. "Don't say anything that will make her upset."

This was Fred Jones. He had recently moved to our overseas site, and his wife wasn't able to cope.

"Fred, your wife doesn't have to have us over for lunch."

"My wife informed me that she will be cooking everything from scratch. She is not a good cook and never cooks anything unless it is in a can, but you guys have made it impossible for her to do that now."

"We don't need to come to your house!"

"You will come to my house, or I will come over to your house and shoot you."

The next day, we went over to Fred's house, and Fred's wife stood in the corner looking quite frazzled. She didn't say anything. We all said "Hi," but she never said a word. She just stood there looking at us. Her face was quite pale, and her hands seemed to tremble.

"Please sit down," Fred said.

We all sat down and Jim exclaimed:

"Will you look at this delicious soup?"

"That is not soup," Fred said. "That is your finger bowl."

From the corner of the room, we could hear a slight stir.

"What's this?" Jim said and held up a huge clump of black hair. "Waiter, there is a bunch of hair in my finger bowl!"

Fred glared at him.

"Oopsie-daisies," Jim said and covered his mouth.

Fred then pointed to the empty plates and told us we had delicious roast beef on our plates.

"Would you like some mashed potatoes?"

We decided, for the sake of Fred's wife, to go ahead and play along with Fred, but Jim wouldn't have any part of it.

"Where's the beef?"

Suddenly, from the corner of the room, Fred's wife leaped out with her hands outstretched as though she wanted to scratch out the eyes of whoever got into her path. We could all see that she was quite mad! Fred quickly got up, and his wife ran into him. They struggled for a while until finally Fred's wife screamed at him:

"Will you please let me go so I can get the roast out of the oven!"

Fred released her and, to our surprise, when she went and opened the oven, there was the most succulent roast that we had ever seen. In fact, we were all amazed that we hadn't smelled it when we walked in the door. There was more than the roast, too! A veritable feast of delicious snow peas, petite carrots, white onions, gravy, salad, and homemade rolls, the likes of which had never been supped on by man or beast.

"This is not a finger bowl," Fred's wife said. "It is a rare Tibetan soup. The hairlike things are imported vegetables."

Fred didn't say anything. He began to rock back and forth. While his wife was busy putting the food on the table, Fred pointed to our empty plates and said:

"The duckling was superb, wasn't it?"

The End

CHRISTMAS CANDLE

The cold winds of November finally beat their way to the massive, wooden door of the church. The crying of the wind outside was equally matched by the placid silence of the empty pews. The barren trees bowed and swayed as if performing a madly, insane dance to the pitiful souls buried beneath the church, in the cellar cemetery. The light of the setting sun caused the shadows on the wall to leap like the very fires of hell trying to devour the wooden lectern, and, not content with that, the building and everything in its path as well.

Nothing could keep out the ray of hope this Christmas Eve. Nothing could stop the onslaught of Christmas piety. Nothing could stop the most Reverend Jenison from locking the Smith family in the church basement.

The Advent wreath—beautiful, elegant, simple—covered with green fir and mistletoe. Four small candles and a larger one in the center adorned the Advent wreath. Every Sunday, one of the small candles was lit by a prominent family of the church until, finally, all the candles were lit with the last remaining candle—the Christmas candle-lit on Christmas morn.

Every year, without fail, the most Reverend Jenison and his family lighted the final candle on Christmas morning. However, the congregation had decided it would be better if this year, instead of Reverend Jenison lighting the candle, a less fortunate couple, with a newborn baby, should be the family to hold the burning wick to the candle.

Although reluctant, the most Reverend Jenison agreed, but his disappointment could plainly be seen on his aged brow.

"I have only one request," Reverend Jenison said, ". . . and that is that the Smith family come and see me first thing on Christmas morning to go over the final candle-lighting procedures."

And, yes, that is exactly what they did, and Reverend Jenison locked them up in the church basement.

When the elegant service began, Reverend Jenison walked graciously up the aisle. The wind howled and crashed against the surface of the old, weather-beaten church. The congregation sat still, solemn, seriously watching the aged pastor crawl up the steps to the lectern.

"It is time to begin," he said with a smile, "Let us have the Smith family come forward and light the Christmas candle to begin our festive occasion."

There was no stirring among the congregation. The howling of the wind and the dashing and crashing of the tree boughs against the pane glass windows were all the congregation heard. But there was another sound. One the congregation did not hear. It was a still, small pounding on the church basement doors.

"Oh, how unfortunate," Reverend Jenison said, ". . . the Smiths are not here to light the candle. The weather must have kept them from coming. Well, I will light the Christmas candle then. I am sorry. It would have been nice to have a young family light the candle."

Right then, there was another pounding—louder than the last. Surely, the congregation must have heard it, but they sat still.

The most Reverend Jenison's hands began to tremble as he took one of the lit candles.

Another pound and another pound and yet another devious pound shook the very fibers of the old church. The congregation did not stir.

"They are mocking me!" Reverend Jenison whispered to himself.

The pounding continued and soon the entire building began to shake and resound from the thunderous, horrible, devilish sounds. The congregation did not move. They were laughing at the pastor. His sin was plain for all to see. His lighting of the

Christmas candle was the end of his reputation and there would be no forgiveness. No room for repentance!

"Enough!" Reverend Jenison suddenly screamed to a very surprised congregation. "Enough of this foul mockery! Enough of this horrible pounding! Here is your precious Smith family. Here they are locked in the basement."

The End

JIM AND THE BOOK

Jim noticed his wife's book had fallen to the floor of the Boeing 707. He picked it up. The book's title was "The Greatest Gift in the Entire World."

"Must be a heartwarming story," Jim thought. He read the opening chapter:

Fred and Frank were friends. They lived in Turkey. Frank had a son born on Turkish soil and wanted to know how Fred had obtained his U.S. Passport for his son while living in Turkey. Fred said that he had to get American passport photos, but he wouldn't recommend that Frank go to this one photographer.

"Why's that?" Frank asked.

"I went to this place and had my son's picture taken, and when I got back the pictures, they were 2 x 1," Fred said.

"What are the U.S. Requirements?" Frank asked.

"2 x 2."

"Did you go back then and get a new set?"

"Yes, but I received back a picture of my wife instead."

"I thought you needed your son's picture?"

"I did."

"What did you do?" Frank said.

"I went back and got more photos taken."

"Did you get a good picture of your son?"

"No, I got back a picture of my son's legs and a picture of my wife's head in front of his body."

"No!"

"Yes, and she was saying something, too," Fred said.

"Really? What was she saying?"

"She was saying . . . er . . . saying . . . one, two, testing . . . one, two . . ."

At this point, Jim noticed that there were a few blank lines and then, in bold type:

IF YOU WOULD LIKE TO KNOW WHAT FRED'S WIFE WAS SAYING, PLEASE TURN TO PAGE 500 OF THIS BOOK!

Jim had a puzzled look on his face. He flipped through the pages. It looked as though the author had lost it all of a sudden. On each page was a scribble or two and finally some figuring of sorts. Around page 300, it looked as if the author were trying to balance his checkbook. The balance was most negative and most of the figuring seemed to indicate that the author didn't have a clue what all the expenses were or what checks were still outstanding.

Jim turned to page 500, and there, nicely centered in the middle of the page, were the words:

"BOOGA BOO!"

Jim couldn't believe this book. It was stupid. Why would his wife buy it? He glanced at the price. It was thirteen dollars! Didn't his wife notice that the book contained worthless, meaningless equations before she had shelled out such a waste of money?

Jim turned to his wife to ask her. She was staring blankly into space with crossed eyes. Her hand was raised high as if holding an imaginary spear. She had a frown on her face.

"Honey?"

"BOOGA BOO!"

The End

MOVIE TIME

When Frank put in a movie system in his home, he went in style. He redesigned his home with a room dedicated to movies. The floors were raised with several rows of plush red chairs. The huge screen had a curtain, and when it opened, the lights would automatically dim. He put in super-surround speakers lined along the acoustically balanced wall to accentuate the one thousand-watt speakers in the front. Everything was fine-tuned to give the ultimate movie watching entertainment experience. He even had a popcorn machine and a soda dispenser.

When his friends arrived, Frank was busy fiddling with the popcorn machine. Somehow, something was stuck in the dispenser, and he was puzzled why. His friends were impressed with the in-home theater and congratulated Frank profusely.

"Yes, but where's the popcorn?" one of the men jokingly said.

"Go and sit down. I'll have popcorn ready by the time you can say 'Jackie Robinson.'"

"Jackie Robinson, Jackie Robinson, Jackie Robinson . . ."

"Funny!" Frank said.

As soon as he saw that his friends were seated, Frank meticulously reached over and with great pomp, turned on the VCR. Suddenly, the sound, the picture, the lighting in the room, played in perfect pitch, and it was only a matter of seconds before Frank's friends actually believed they were in a high-class movie theater. And right when the effect was making Frank's friends give him the bragging rights of the year, Frank turned off the movie.

"Anybody for raisins?" he asked. "Only fifty cents a box."

Frank had a box, and he was tipping it to let everyone see that he had enough raisins for everyone if they wanted. Some of the raisins fell out of the box.

"Okay, Frank," Tom said. "Okay, Frank. I'll take one."

"That'll be fifty cents."

Tom handed over two quarters, and Frank quickly ran and put them in a toy cash register.

"Ding! Ding!" Frank said.

"Are you going to start the movie again?" one of his friends asked.

"I might," Frank said. He then sauntered over, kind of humming, and looked around the room. Then, with greater pomp than before, Frank pushed the little play button on the machine and the little red button at the same time.

"I can record over my movies, too!"

"Frank, don't do that; that was a good movie!" Mike said.

Frank stopped the machine and ejected the tape.

"Yeah, well, I don't particularly care for it. I'll be right back. I have another tape I think you'll like."

A few minutes later, Frank stuck his head around the corner and asked whether anyone wanted a pickle.

"How much this time?" asked one of his friends. Everyone laughed.

"Forty-five cents. And I expect payment upon delivery!"

"You're kidding! You are going to charge us for pickles, too?" Tom suddenly asked.

"I'm going to charge you for the movie as well!" Frank said. Frank's friends suddenly began to lose interest in Frank's new movie theater.

"I think it is time to go," Joe said and started to get up.

"Oh, sit down, Joe!" Frank said. "The pickles and the movie are free! I was just kidding."

Joe started to say something but before he could, Frank walked over and stuck a big old pickle in his mouth.

"I'll get the money from you before you leave," Frank whispered.

Frank ran off, and for a few minutes, the room was quiet. Frank's friends looked around the room to see whether Frank was going to reappear, but there was no sign of him.

"Maybe he left?" one of his ex-friends said.

"I hope he has!" someone said. "Let's leave!"

Suddenly, the loudspeakers began to blare out:

"Samuel Jacoby was a humanitarian before his time. Today we have the rare privilege of continuing his great humanitarian work. Let's not let him down. Contribute to the Samuel Jacoby Memorial Fund!"

Frank appeared as a cowboy and slapped his knee.

"Put 'er thar, pardner!" Frank said and passed out a huge popcorn bucket. His friends, feeling guilty, reached into their pockets and threw in a few pennies. Frank wasn't pleased with the amount, but he decided he would charge them double for the movie.

"Frank? Are we going to see anything?"

"Yeah that is what you would like, isn't it? Sam Jacoby wasn't a good enough cause for you to stop and think about the great work that is needed in our world today. All you want to do is watch a movie."

Right then, the popcorn machine began to act up. It was popping way too much corn. Frank ran and checked the machine to see why it was doing so. Instead of one cup, Frank had put in one bucket. Frank pulled the plug, but the machine was too hot. The corn began to pop even more frantically and started to spill out onto the concession floor.

"No, this can't be!" Frank screamed.

Suddenly, the popcorn machine exploded and popcorn spewed all over the place. The explosion blew Frank's video machine across the room. The commotion that suddenly started in the movie room was nothing compared with Frank trying to dig himself out of the popcorn. With so much popcorn, Frank was barely able to get the doors open.

"May . . . may . . . I have your attention, please," Frank said.

Everyone turned to stare at Frank. He had butter and a big bucket of popcorn on top of his head.

"Please watch your step!"

Frank's ex-friends got up in a huff. As they stormed out, they realized too late the neon exit signs were above fake doors cleverly painted on the walls and smashed right into them!

The End

THE CAMERA STORY

"The reason I gathered you here today," Big Boss Jim Bob said, " is to plot a new strategy to sell our photographic equipment. In the guise of a professional, objective magazine, we will sell our complete line of cameras. Rave about them, give them full coverage, rate them high by reader polls. Of course, the only readers to be polled will be you, the employees of this company. And, we must disguise this magazine in such a way as to not let anyone know our intentions. Not even one hint or smidgen of crass commercialization."

"Uh . . . like, maybe put a recipe in the magazine?" Sally asked.

"Yes, yes, something like that. Make it a really wholesome, family magazine." Jim Bob replied.

"Like . . . a recipe for crepe suzettes?" Sally asked.

"Yeah . . . yeah, beautiful, something like that. Go ahead and put in a recipe for crepe suzettes," Jim Bob said.

All together the employees said: "We'll get to it right away, boss."

Within a few weeks, the magazine was ready. Sally came and presented it to big boss Jim Bob.

"Here's the new magazine, sir."

"Hmmm, let me see," Jim said eager to review it. "Why . . . why, the cover of a scuba diver is brilliant. Yes . . . let's see. Oh, I see that the recipe for crepe suzettes is splashed on pages one and two . . . page three . . . and page four . . . six . . . and here's an ad for a garage sale at Joe's. Very good, real family-like."

Jim flipped through the remainder of the magazine with less than an enthusiastic manner.

"And . . . another recipe for crepe suzettes," he said.

"We got a recipe from everyone in the office," Sally replied.

Suddenly, in a moment of realization, Joe closed the magazine. He pointed to the scuba diver.

"What does scuba diving have to do with a magazine about crepe suzettes?" Joe asked.

"Uh . . . " Sally said.

"How do you expect to sell any crepes this way?" Joe demanded.

"Uh . . . uh . . ."

"Well?"

Sally suddenly threw one of the company's cameras at Joe.

"Say 'CHEESE SOUFFLE'!" she yelled.

The End

PINK, FLUFFY CLOUDS

Too much fluff! There was way too much fluff in the clouds. They were pink! Over the mountains you could see them coming. Big, pink, fluffy clouds. Full of snow. All of them! It was too late to get into the car and leave town. They were going to have to stay and let all the clouds go and do their business on top of their heads. No one was safe. No one but Jerry who sat behind his keyboard writing important business messages to folks back home.

"Are you sure you want to stay?" Mike asked him.

"No fluffy cloud is going to make me go home early!" said Jerry and those were his last words on the subject.

Mike sat looking out the window with his nose pressed hard against the pane. He looked up into the sky and watched the clouds accumulate. One of the clouds was particularly ominous and was hovering over Jerry's car.

"Jerry?" Mike said.

"Don't you have any work to do?" Jerry asked him, annoyed at all the hoopla over pink, fluffy clouds.

Mike didn't say a word and watched the clouds continue their downward trek from the mountains. And soon, before too long and not too late after that either, the snow began to fall. And it fell with a great roar and crash. Snow everywhere. Hitting cars, pedestrians, anything that moved, and even little fluffy rabbits hopping around in the meadow.

Mike looked nervously around the room. He wanted to say something to his boss, but he was scared. His boss's car was now being completely buried by the blizzard. The wind was blowing against the windows so much that they rattled back and forth. The cold wind found cracks in the panes so that the heat in the room couldn't compete. But Jerry didn't care. All he did was sit even closer to his computer and work as though it was a fine spring day.

"Don't make an issue of it," Jerry told Mike when he noticed him becoming increasingly agitated. "The storm will subside and the snow will melt before we go home."

Mike again looked out the window and saw the temperature gauge dropping rapidly. The snow was not showing any signs of slowing and there were more pink, fluffy clouds coming over the mountains.

"I'm leaving!" Mike screamed.

Jerry looked up at him in disgust.

The windows began to crack as the snow piled higher and higher creating enormous bearing pressure on the plate-glass. The wind howled and shrieked. The pink fluffy clouds were now ravenous monsters devouring anything and anyone in their paths.

Jerry didn't notice him leaving. He continued to absorb himself in the mundane task of looking up part numbers while the weather continued to twist, contort, and do all sort of nasty things. Mike barely made it home alive, but once inside his nice, warm, cozy house, he breathed a sigh of deep relief.

However, for Jerry, it was a different story. After the clock struck five o'clock and he had turned off his computer, Jerry put on his coat and walked outside. And then it happened. The snow had accumulated so much that a huge snowball had formed on the roof. As soon as Jerry had walked outside and slammed the door, the snowball promptly fell off the roof and landed square smack on Jerry's head.

Jerry didn't say much after he cleared the snow off his head. He just skipped across the parking lot looking for his car, and not finding it, he skipped across the street to the factory to look up some more parts. Once inside, he skipped down the aisles and skipped out the back where more snow had accumulated.

Jerry decided to skip back into the factory, but another clump of snow fell and blocked the entrance. Jerry didn't notice that pinker, fluffier clouds were forming right over his head. He didn't notice that the wind had picked up and that freezing sleet was beginning to pelt him. All he noticed was that he wasn't finished skipping for the day and, therefore, would skip around through the snow, through the freezing rain, and through any pink, fluffy cloud that might just happen to be in his way during his marathon skip.

"I really don't understand why no one else is outside skipping? It is a beautiful day."

Just when he said this, another ton of snow fell off the roof and buried Jerry to his waist. Of course, it landed on his head before it fell to the ground and buried him up to his waist. There was no reaction from Jerry.

"I will climb every mountain. Reach for every star," he said.

And with those very words, Jerry skipped off to the mountains in the blinding snowstorm, never to be seen or heard from again. (Until work the next day, that is.)

The End

PEDRO'S SURPRISE

The summer heat had been merciless. The sun's heat had intensified so much that it had evaporated the very oceans and formed huge clouds across the planet.

Pedro was quite amazed at all this. He began to walk into the dry ocean bed to see if he could find any trace of water, but all he found was dead fish and huge whalebones.

Finally, right in the center of the ocean, Pedro felt a drop of rain.

Hallelujah! The drought was over at last!

The End

HOW WE OBTAINED OUR RABBIT SKIN RUG, OR WHY ANIMALS ARE EXTINCT

You see, it was like this. My wife and I decided we would go and spend the day in the local zoo. It was a beautiful spring day. Much like three years ago.

We walked by the rabbit cage and my wife immediately began to get nervous.

"Look at his ears," she said.

I ignored her remark, but apparently she couldn't forget.

"He's going to escape and he is going to come to our house. You have to do something about it," she told me.

"He's in a cage," I said. "There is no way he is going to escape."

And now, this is how we met Joe. He was a wry, old man. His bony hand reached out ever so gently to touch mine when I greeted him.

"What may I do for you," he asked.

"You need to get rid of that rabbit," I said. "It's scaring my wife."

"That rabbit wouldn't hurt a flea," Joe said.

"That rabbit is going to escape tonight!"

"What do you want me to do?" Joe laughingly said. "Go over there and kill it?"

The next day, Joe was at our doorsteps pounding on the door.

"Honey, it's the curator of the zoo," I said. "Hello, Joe, did you have a pleasant sleep?"

Joe's eyes popped out when he saw the rabbit skin rug promptly displayed in our house.

"My rabbit!"

"I told you yesterday that rabbit was scaring my wife," I said.

"You killed my rabbit!"

"Yes, I did."

"Joe, I noticed you had some baby seals in your zoo," my wife said. "I'm afraid they're going to escape. Please kill them."

"Do you need any help with that?" I asked. "In fact, why don't we kill all the animals."

". . . and little Fi-Fi down the street," my wife interjected.

"I'll get my gun."

"You can't get away with this," Joe said. "I'm calling the police."

"I don't think so," I said. "If you go to the police, we will have to club you with the seals."

"You . . . you folks need help," Joe said. "What possible legitimate reason can you have for committing such an atrocity."

"We're hungry."

There was a moment of silence. Joe looked at his watch. It was almost noon. Time for lunch.

"Let's move out," Joe said.

"I'll bring the salt and pepper," my wife said.

The End

WRITER'S BLOCK!

It was no use! Frank was sitting at his desk looking at a blank page on his favorite word processing program. He couldn't think. He had no original ideas. He was absolutely stupid. There was a deadline and he was totally unable to meet it.

His hands began to tremble as he sat staring.

"Gotta think," he said.

Frank's wife walked into the study.

"Don't you think you need to be getting to bed?"

"I can't. I have to write a story and put it on the Internet. The Americans will be up in a few hours. My readers will be disappointed if they don't find a new story to read."

"Frank, this is only a hobby," Jill told her husband. "You aren't being paid to do this."

"Wait . . . I am getting a thought. Yes, it is coming. Wait. Wait," Frank said.

"Well, I am going to bed," Jill said. "Please don't stay up too long."

Frank sat still after she left. His mind was blank again. There was nothing more that he could do. He decided that he had better follow his wife's advice again and go on to bed.

And then, as it normally seems to happen to men in Frank's position, a small 4.5 earthquake occurred off the Sea of Japan and shook the apartment building, but it had little effect on its structural integrity. However, the bookshelf beside Frank had a nice size book sitting strategically on top. And when the earthquake had subsided, this book was sitting on top of Frank's head.

In the morning, Jill woke up and was startled to see that her husband's side of the bed was untouched. She got up out of bed, put on her robe, and went into the study. She was surprised to see her husband still staring at a blank screen. She was equally surprised to see a huge book on top of his head.

"Frank?" Jill asked.

"You know," Frank said, "you can absorb a lot of information like this. Did you know that energy is neither created nor destroyed and $e=mc^2$?"

It was then that Jill realized that their son's science book was sitting on top of Frank's head. Curious, she replaced it with the family Bible.

"The Lord is my shepherd, I shall not want . . . " Frank continued.

Jill replaced the Bible with a CD on the world's greatest operas. Frank immediately broke into an aria.

"Frank," Jill suddenly said excitedly, "I have an idea!"

Frank stopped singing long enough to listen to his wife—something he had not done in years. Jill explained her scheme. She would take down various books from the bookshelf and place them on top of Frank's head. Whatever thoughts entered into his mind, he should type them down. By carefully choosing the books, Frank should be able to whip out several great short stories.

Frank was beside himself. The plan was brilliant. He put his hands to the keyboard like a concert pianist.

"Let the melody begin!" he said.

"Let's see if this will help you with your spelling," said Jill as she placed a large dictionary on Frank's head.

Frank began to type furiously.

"A bee can drink even four glasses heartily inside jumping kittens leaping merrily now on . . ." Frank typed.

Jill yanked the book off Frank's head. He had just alphabetically typed a string of gibberish. His hands went limp at the keyboard, and his eyes held a vacant stare. Jill placed a book of Shakespeare's plays on Frank's head.

"To be or not to be Romeo," Frank wrote with great finesse. "That is the question. Whether 'tis more noble in mind to be a fair prince."

"Out! Out! Foul prince!" Juliet screamed.

"I come not to steal away your heart," Romeo replied. "So I shalt hide from your lovely face."

"Wherefore art thou, Romeo?"

Jill looked at what Frank had written. Not only was he writing a horrible love story, but also he was grossly misinterpreting everything Shakespeare wrote. She quickly substituted Shakespeare with the "World's Greatest Fairy Tales".

"And they got married after the wicked queen stepmother was dead and lived happily ever after. The End," Frank wrote.

He looked up at Jill. She had really come through this time. He had written a masterpiece and now he could publish it on the World Wide Web where everyone with access to the Internet could read it.

"Frank, I think it needs a little more polishing."

"Nonsense, child," Frank said. "I will publish it right away!"

"I said it needs more POLISHING!" Jill screamed as she banged a book entitled "How to Polish Silverware, Brassware and Copperware" on top of Frank's head.

"You're right, it DOES need more polishing."

Frank got up from the computer and went to the kitchen. When he returned, he brought back a bottle of silverware polish and began to smear it all over their brand new special edition $9,000 computer.

"No!" Jill screamed. "That is not what I meant!"

She quickly took the book on "How to Love Your Computer as Your Wife" and placed it on his head. Fortunately for Jill, Frank adored his wife and suddenly saw the errors of his way.

"Oh, forgive me. I am so sorry," Frank said.

"That's okay," Jill said. "I don't think you hurt our computer."

"I love you so much," Frank said, caressing and kissing the computer screen. "Would you care for a little more polish my dear?"

Frank started pouring the polish on the keyboard.

"Hey, this should really give our stories a shine now!"

Jill couldn't believe it. She quickly placed a book on etiquette on top of his head.

"Oh, did I polish your keys too hard? I am sorry. It was so rude of me," Frank said to the keyboard.

Jill grabbed the keyboard before Frank could do any more damage.

"Hey!" Frank screamed. "Don't hurt my baby!"

"Your baby?" Jill screamed back. "You are beginning to act as stupid as your stories!"

Suddenly, Jill realized that instead of a book on etiquette, she had placed the book "The Adventures of Mr. Stupidhead" on top of her husband's head.

Frank pointed to the goldfish bowl.

"Do you know what type of fish those are?" he said.

"Why they are ordinary goldfish," Jill said.

"No, they aren't. They are flying fish," Frank said and went over to the bowl, picked up some fish and threw them across the room. "See the fishies fly!"

"Frank!" Jill screamed and quickly ran to save the fish.

"Oh yeah," Frank said, "the stories are flowing now. Yes sir."

Frank took some of the silver polish and began to use it like finger paint on the screen.

"The Flying Fish," he wrote, "by Mr. Stupidhead."

And, as Jill was putting the fish back into the bowl, Frank's writer's block was miraculously cured, and the ideas and the silver polish began to flow like streams of fresh mountain water running over rocks and fresh green moss through forests where, in the distance, the woodpecker played its normal tune and the smell of pines was eagerly greeted by early morning mountain hikers.

"I've got a million of 'em, folks!" Frank said.

The End

NEW YORK

All his life, Al had dreamed of earning enough money to move out of his small hick town and move to New York. Every day, after school, Al would work long hours at the local grocery store, stocking shelves, cleaning floors, and running the cash register.

Finally, high school graduation day arrived. Everyone was shaking Al's hand or slapping him on the back, telling him what a fine boy he was. Mr. Smith, the grocery store owner, walked up to him, beaming.

"I'm mighty proud of you, Al," he said. "I've been wanting to tell you something for quite a while now but decided to wait until your graduation day. Al, I'm offering you a partnership in my business. What do you think, boy?"

Everyone oohed and aahed, saying what a great opportunity this was and how generous of Mr. Smith. As for Al, he had never been so insulted in all his life. To think that everyone would think that he would stay in this small hick town any longer than necessary. He had the money saved up now and was itching to board the bus to New York, his dream city.

"Thanks but no thanks," Al answered abruptly. "If you think that I'm going to stay in this one horse town a minute longer with all you small-minded people, you've got another thing coming!"

With their shocked and hurt faces looking at him, Al boarded the bus to New York. When he got there, he had a quick look around.

"Hmmm, it's not exactly what I expected. Oh well, I guess I'll go back home now," Al said as he boarded the bus back home.

The End

THE LANGUAGE TUTOR

They had great hopes for the future. They were going to be missionaries to an Asian country. They figured learning the language would be a breeze since they were astute students. When they arrived and began language class, the instructor, instead of speaking a word of English, began to put up odd shaped letters on the board.

"Dfdsf fdsfdsfdsafsd gfdghgfshggfhdh gfdgfdf," he droned on in a monotonous tone.

He kept on writing more odd-shaped letters on the blackboard. He never turned around to face his students. No one in the classroom could understand. He kept on droning on and on in a monotonous tone, "Dfdsfa fdsfdafdsa fdafdsafd fdsafdsafd."

The Kraddocks were stupefied.

"I think we should find ourselves a new language tutor," Mr. Kraddock said to his wife.

The next day, instead of going to the mission board's exclusive training class for the elite, the Kraddocks had Mr. Chongmmmmm-mmm as their language tutor.

"Mr. Chong," Mr. Kraddock said, "we hope you can help us learn the language quickly."

"Mr. Chongmmmmm-mmm is my name," Mr. Chongmmmmm-mmm said. "Please say it correctly before we began."

The Kraddocks tried for an hour to say his last name, but they were totally stupefied.

"I will go and find students more qualified for my elite services," Mr. Chongmmmmm-mmm said.

The Kraddocks begged Mr. Chongmmmmm-mmm to change his name to Mr. Chong so he could be their language tutor, but he had never heard of such nonsense.

When he left, the Kraddocks were very sad.

"Maybe we should go back to class," Mrs. Kraddock said.

"MAYBE we should quit," Mr. Kraddock said. "Let's go back to the mission board tomorrow and turn in our resignation."

Mrs. Kraddock was surprised at her husband's sudden change of mind.

"What about all the money and gifts people gave us before we came over here to encourage us in our missionary endeavors?" Mrs. Kraddock asked.

"We'll tell them the truth," Mr. Kraddock said. "The devil doesn't want us here—period!"

The next day, the Kraddocks went before the mission board with their resignation.

"The devil doesn't want us here," Mr. Kraddock said.

"The devil doesn't want any of us here!" the head missionary said. "Haven't you ever heard of spiritual warfare?"

"Yes, but the devil particularly doesn't want us here," Mr. Kraddock emphasized.

"Nonsense," the head missionary said. "You can learn the language if you really put your heart to it. God gives wisdom abundantly to those who ask . . . "

"Huh?" Mrs. Kraddock said.

"You need to ask God for wisdom?" the head missionary said.

Mr. Kraddock looked like a light had gone off in his head.

"I . . . I . . . I," he said.

"Why don't you two pray about it and go to class tomorrow and see what happens," the head missionary said.

"God will move if you seek to glorify Him."

The next day, after praying that God would bless them and make them the best students in the entire language institute so that others would notice how proficient they were in another language and heap praise upon them, the Kraddocks walked into the language institute. Much to their relief and praise, the Kraddocks learned that the old language teacher had left.

Unfortunately, much to their anxiety and distress, their new teacher was Mr. Chongmmmmm-mmm.

"Please say my name before we begin class." Mr. Chongmmmmm-mmm said to the students. Not one person in the classroom could pronounce his name correctly. Mr. Chongmmmmm-mmm told everyone in the class that they would never be able to learn the language if they couldn't pronounce a simple name. Many of the students began to cry.

"Look!" Mr. Kraddock said. "Every name in this country is one syllable long. Mr. Wu. Mr. Wong. No one is called Mr. Chongmm-mmmm, uh, Chongm-mmm, uh . . ."

"Well, I never!" Mr. Chongmmmmm-mmm said. "I refuse to waste another minute of my time."

"No! This is stupid!" Mr. Kraddock said, rising to his feet, "I don't really think your name is what you say it is!"

"Oh," Mr. Chongmmmmm-mmm said, "and what is my real name?"

"Beelzebub!" Mr. Kraddock said. "You are the devil! Lucifer!"

"What?" Mr. Chongmmmmm-mmm said, suddenly looking quite agitated. "Nonsense."

"Yeah," Mr. Kraddock said. "I think you are wearing a mask."

Mr. Chongmmmmm-mmm began to back away.

"A mask?"

Mr. Kraddock went to pull at his face, but, before he could do so, Mr. Chongmmmmm-mmm suddenly transformed into a hideous creature and then vanished with a dazzling display of fire and smoke.

"Mr. Chongmmmm-mmm really was the devil!" Mr. Kraddock said. "Hey! I can say his name!"

"Dfdsfa fdsfdafdsa fdafdsafd fdsafdsafd," Mrs. Kraddock and the students replied in a monotonous tone. "Dfdsfa fdsfdafdsa fdafdsafd fdsafdsafd."

The End

THE NEWLYWEDS

Charlotte woke up early to make breakfast for her new husband. She walked into the kitchen and tripped over some dishes that her husband had refused to wash.

"Up early?" Frank asked, sipping a hot cup of coffee and reading the paper.

"Going to get you some breakfast, honey," Charlotte said and went over to the icebox.

"I suppose you want something good?" Charlotte said.

"I really don't eat anything for breakfast, dear," Frank said.

Charlotte took out a few eggs and then deliberately dropped them at his feet.

"I suppose you won't clean that up either," she said.

"Look, if you don't know how to cook eggs, just say you don't know," Frank said.

"If you wouldn't just sit there but help me, everything would be a lot better."

"I don't think so," Frank said.

"Oh, and I suppose you can make a better breakfast than me?" Charlotte said.

"Well," Frank said, "I am the head chef at the Françoise."

"Oh, so that makes you the prince of fine cookery?"

"Well, no, actually it makes me its king."

At that very moment, the doors opened and royal courtiers walked in and put a regal robe on Frank and a crown on his head.

Charlotte had no choice but to bow.

The End

THE LOVELY BRIDE

It was in the wintertime. The lovely icicles of frozen water languidly hung mid-air from the tundrid rooftops where peaks of white, puffy snow had accumulated with the seasonable, nighttime freeze.

The pink clouds had been a sign, indeed. For Phillipe, and his lovely-to-be bride, Beatrice, were going to be coalesced into a blissful connubialation of matrimonial harmony.

Phillipe was the Ying and his lovely bride the Yang. It was going to be a Yang good time for all involved with a wild Ying afterwards. Phillipe even thought the entire affair had a ripe, good, old Ying to it as he thought how he was going to take his fleeting bachelorhood and Yang it out to dry for good.

"Yang it all to Ying," Phillipe verbalized looking staid. "I simply cannot go through with this espousal!"

Beatrice looked out the window into the stupendous spectacle of summits of sparkling snow. The sun luminesced on the frozen lake where a few ice-skaters slowly glided on what looked like glistening glass.

"What a day to be married," Beatrice tittered, flinging her arms above her head in sheer delectation.

She looked at her wedding gown lying on her bed. The tailors had done a prodigious job of designing the perfect winter gown. White satin trimmed in white fox fur flowed over the edge of her bed onto the floor. She knew that Phillipe would love the way she would look in it as much as she would love the way he would look in the matching white satin tuxedo trimmed in the same fur. Their matching fur hats would emblematize the plenary match that their lives had become and would be. As Phillipe had so aptly put it, they were Ying and Yang, Yang and Ying.

Beatrice went over to her rigging and caressed it genteelly. She had wanted to be mated for so long that she simply couldn't transgress all the felicity in her. She let out a spacious whoop and pirouetted around the room in great fruition and exhilaration.

"I am to be nuptialed to Phillipe! Phillipe! Phillipe!"

She footed it around and around with such jubilation that she failed to see the wardrobe dresser in her spinning artery. Suddenly, with little forewarning, Beatrice hammered into the wardrobe and fell in such a technique as to hit her head promptly on the hardened floor.

"Eeeerrrrrr," she said. "Eeeeerrr, I am going to wear my gown on my head like a turban. I am too!"

Outside the window, the snow began to plummet balmily in billows of blustering bales. Phillipe looked petulantly at it and wrung his hands, deprecating his situation. How was he going to tell Beatrice that their marriage was derision, a story never to be told! He looked at the doltish excuse for wedding attire hanging in his closet. Beatrice had insisted on designing it with a winter flair. He was sure that Beatrice's wedding gown would make her look more at home with Robert Perry at the North Pole than with the minister in the chapel. The matching fur hats made them look like they had dead baby seals sitting on their heads.

"That's it," Phillipe cried, "I'll call the Animal Lover's Society and tell them that Beatrice had our hats made of baby seal fur. Their investigation should delay the wedding long enough for me to make my getaway!"

Phillipe simpered fiendishly at his ingenious plan.

"Oh, goody gumdrops," Beatrice said and curtseyed and danced with each falling angel teardrop softly bashing against the purple window panes and the pulchritudinous tinted green glass which she spent a thousand dollars to install—the very glass, indeed, that Phillipe had argued with her for oh such a long time until she finally told him to go and pick out the glass to go with the silken Chinese curtains.

"Yes," she said, composing herself in the key of *e* flat, " Phillipe gets me and my luscious body, too!"

And then, ravenously and salivating all over the place, Beatrice growled out loud:

"I AM A LOVELY BRIDE! LOOK AT ME!!"

Without a moment's hesitation, Phillipe quickly dialed the Animal Lover's Society to tell them about the baby seal fur hats.

"Hello, Animal Lover's Society," a beauteous feminine voice answered. "May I help you?"

Phillipe was so taken aback by the resplendent sound of this voice that he was ephemerally speechless and even elided why he had made this phone call. Suddenly, all he wanted to do was meet the woman from whom issued this euphonious diapason.

"Er, yes," Phillipe stammered, searching his confused mind for something to say. "Do you have Prince Albert in a can?"

"No," the woman replied quite seriously. "This is the Animal Lover's Society. We only have animals here."

"Well, then let him out," Phillipe guffawed, quite out of control. The woman chortled, too, in a hysterical sort of way.

"That's my favorite joke," she laughed. "You've really livened up an otherwise dull and boring day. My name is Sophie. What's yours?"

"Phillipe," Phillipe replied. "Say, what time do you get off? I'd like to meet you, maybe go out to dinner? By the way, what do you think of a winter wedding?"

Sophie was taken aback by the precipitousness of the events which were unfolding before her very eyes, or ears, should we say. She never dreamt that when she awoke this morning that she would be blessed with a proposal from a complete stranger. Her eyes drifted out to the miraculous scene outside the window, and she thanked the invisible stars for her convivial fortune.

Meanwhile, back at the ranch, Beatrice was beating her brains out trying to get into her turban costume.

"Eeeerrrr," she said, "Eeeeeerrrr. Kick! One, two, three, kick!"

She struggled and straggled with her wedding gown, sequins popping off and flying all over the place. Her white, snowshoe high heels skidded all over the polished porcelain tiles of her ballroom bedroom resplendent with a huge, immoderate, glinting chandelier hanging high off the floor, almost thirty feet or so.

"I . . . want. . . to . . . get . . . this . . . outfit . . . on . . . so . . . bad," she said, "that . . . I . . . can . . . feel . . . it!"

"EEEEE, EEEE, EEEE!" she screamed. "EEEE! Help me, help me!"

Beatrice barked and whimpered, clutching her wedding gown and clawing at the ruffled skirts to be put on her head, upside down so that the wedding skirt would flow over her head like cascading waterwheels of delicious merry-go-around, white, puffy, scrumptious cotton candy.

"Mmmmm-mmm," Beatrice said and licked her lips at the thought of cotton candy. "I sure am hungry, now! Mmmm-mm-mmm."

"Sophie, Sophie, are you still there?" Phillipe mused.

Sophie sat staring into sediment of space. "What. . . what time do we eat dinner?" she catechized.

"I've changed my mind, Sophie," Phillipe retorted. "I love Beatrice."

Phillipe hung up the phone.

Sophie was crushed. What had turned out to be a wonderful dream suddenly turned into a nightmare. Phillipe had solicited her out on a date and then had renegaded. Her life was undone.

"I will let all the animals free," she said. "It's the least I can do."

Beatrice sat on her bed and gloated at herself in the mirror. She looked like a water fountain.

"I hope Phillipe is pleased," she articulated.

Phillipe sat looking at his desk.

"I don't want to get married today," he said. "I think I will go to the zoo."

Phillipe got up and walked outside.

Suddenly, a lion from the Animal Lover's Society jumped on him and ate him alive.

Moral:

It is better to be in the belly of a lion than in the hands of a jilted bride.

The End

THE NEW COMPUTER

Veronica stared dejectedly at the new computer that her husband had bought. After years of buying and using only the top of the line models from the most elite computer company, her husband went out and bought an off brand. An off brand! She started to write down her thoughts in what she thought was a word processing program when the phone rang. It was her husband, wondering how he could speed up the computer even more.

Veronica was dumbfounded. He had only had the computer less than 24 hours, and he was already dissatisfied with some of its features. Veronica packed the computer neatly in its original box and shipped it to a space center where it was loaded onto the next commercial rocket, thereby finally reaching its maximum speed in outer space.

"Now, it's the fastest computer in the world. In fact, it's out of this world!" said Veronica.

When Mike came home and heard what his wife had done, he had only one thing to say:

"Outta sight."

The End

THE KISS

"Chara Lee," Dr. Jones, Professor of Literature at Carroll County Junior College said. "I believe you need a little more help with your writing skills."

"Why, isn't it a good story?" Mrs. Chara Lee Whittier said.

"Well, I think you were trying to tell a simple story about a couple's first kiss on a beach," Professor Jones said. "That's all very well, however, you let other things clutter up your story."

"What do you mean?" Chara Lee asked.

Professor Jones read the first paragraphs:

Jill, in a paisley dress, with a beautiful blue bonnet and a matching blue ribbon, took a sip of soda and looked at Joe through the soda glass. Joe took a sip of her soda and let a little of it dribble down his chin. He watched the sun set on the water. The clouds were beautiful and pink. One of the clouds looked like a duck.

"Quack, quack," Joe said.

Jill took out the checkbook and began to write some checks to pay off some bills. Her checkbook had a paisley cover. It matched her dress. She took a sip of soda.

Joe took another sip of soda, too.

Jill was hungry and decided to order something.

The professor stopped.

"What's this?"

"What's what?" Chara Lee said.

"What's all this nonsense about clothes and clouds?"

"I think clothes and clouds add something to a story," Chara Lee said.

"They add nothing to a story about someone kissing another person," the professor said, "I want you to rewrite it, keeping that in mind."

The next day, Professor Jones was shaking his head.

"This is a rewrite?" he asked.

Joe was quacking so much that Jill told him that they should put the food order on his bill. Jill was writing checks so fast that Joe's head was dizzy. He staggered to collect their delectable prized turkey with all the trimmings. The turkey dropped to the sand and the stuffing spilt out.

"I'm going to quack-up," Jill said, her blue ribbon flowing in the breeze.

"This is trash!" Professor Jones said. "What East Coast college did you say you went to?"

Chara Lee was insulted.

"How dare you talk to me in that manner," she said. "Don't you appreciate avant-garde writing when you see it?"

"Avant-garde?" Professor Jones said. "This is avant-garde?"

"I think it is a new style of writing," Chara Lee said. "I can't believe you don't like it."

"Well, let me make one thing clear," Professor Jones said. "No one is going to want to read this story past the second paragraph. This is not avant-garde writing. This is insane! In fact, in my opinion, after I read this, I think Joe is insane and I have serious doubts about Jill's frame of mind, too! Why do I care if they kiss or not since they are nothing but a bunch of raving lunatics?"

Chara Lee said, "I'll try to make it a little more believable, then."

The following morning, Professor Jones received the following on his desk:

"Quack, quack, quack," Joe said flapping his arms. "Put the food on my bill."

"You wanna see bills, I'll show you bills," Jill said waving her afternoon mail in his face.

Joe, wearing a paisley shirt and a blue ribbon around his head, pointed to the clouds.

Jill pointed to her checkbook.

Joe pointed to the soda bottle.

Jill pointed to the spilt turkey.

Professor Jones pointed the paper towards the paper shredder. He then placed the shredding in an envelope and wrote "REWRITE" in red. He placed this outside his door and went to lunch.

Chara Lee was quite angry to receive her "final" rewrite in pieces. Professor Jones had no business to do this. She would not let him get away with this. She would take revenge.

Her friend Elaine was no help. Chara Lee had taken the course because her husband had laughed at her when she said only Ivy League schools were the best academically. He had challenged her to take a similar literary writing course at a local Junior College.

"I can't believe you are doing that bad," Elaine said. "You used to be an excellent writer."

"I don't know. I guess I lost it somewhere," Chara Lee said.

"Well, why don't you show Professor Jones some of your old work and see if he can suggest where you went wrong," Elaine said.

Chara Lee smiled. Of course, her old works! Why not submit one of her old "A+" college stories. It really wasn't cheating. She had written them herself.

Professor Jones met Chara Lee at the door the next day with a paper shredder.

"Put it in there."

"How dare you!" Chara Lee said. "You haven't even read my rewrite."

"I'm sure it needs to be shredded and rewritten again," Professor Jones said.

"Please, Professor Jones, just give me another chance! Please read my 'newly' rewritten story," Chara Lee said.

"Oh, very well, if I must," Professor Jones said. He took her paper and read it aloud:

Little hopping bunny rabbit hopped all around. He was sure no one was going to catch him in Farmer McGarver's vegetable garden.

Professor Jones dropped the paper—the only copy that Chara Lee had—into the paper shredder and turned it on.

"My paper!" Chara Lee screamed.

"What does a bunny have to do with a romantic kiss?" Professor Jones said.

"My Ivy League grade 'A+' paper," Chara Lee said.

"Rewrite."

"My little hopping bunny rabbit paper."

"Rewrite your story and don't waste my time by bringing any more Ivy League dribble!" Professor Jones said.

Chara Lee couldn't believe it. How was she going to pass this course? She had already rewritten her paper three times.

When Chara Lee got home, Mike greeted her, waving an envelope in his hand.

"I just had to open this letter and pry into your personal life, " Mike said. " You've been requested to submit an old bunny story for immediate publication in a children's anthology."

"My old bunny story?" Chara Lee said.

"One of your old college professors remembered how great this story was that you wrote in college and suggested that it be included," Mike said. "If they like it, they'll give you one thousand dollars to publish it! Wow!"

"My old bunny story?" Chara Lee said.

"I didn't think you were that good of a writer," Mike said, "but if it gets us a thousand dollars, you must be something."

"My old bunny story?" Chara Lee said.

"I guess that Junior College course is pretty boring to such a gifted writer like you," Mike said.

The next day Chara Lee was in despair.

"It's no use," Chara Lee told Elaine, "I've lost it. I can't think. Those stupid Ivy League schools didn't teach me a thing!"

Elaine put her arm around her.

"Don't you say that. I know you. You will be able to whip one out in no time!"

"Do you really think so?"

"Would I lie to you?"

Both women laughed, and Chara Lee snorted.

Several hours later she was gleaming.

Hop. Little Bunny. Paisley skies and beach puff pies. Don't you worry little bunny. Hopping through the woods!

"Perfect!" Chara Lee said and quickly sealed the story in an envelope and mailed it off to her professors.

"Chara Lee! Don't you think that you need to wait and rewrite it?" Elaine asked her.

Chara Lee Whittier, who had all of a sudden turned quite snobby and haughty since she had received the offer from her Ivy League professors, laughed at her narrow-minded friend.

"Be off. I hear your momma crying," she said with a laugh.

Elaine couldn't believe her ears.

"Well, I never!" Elaine left in a huff.

"Who needs little people like her when I have the elite?" Chara Lee said and sat on the couch like a queen. "I do so hope that no-good husband of mine will quickly return from his mundane job to fetch me a glass of water."

A few weeks later, Chara Lee received a letter in the mail from the professors' writing committee. She tossed it in the trash without reading it and quickly called them.

"How dare you send me a letter! I will not discuss anything with you but in person."

"But . . . " her old professor said.

"No 'buts', Professor," she said. "I will send you and your colleagues first class airline tickets. Come to my story acceptance award supper this Saturday night."

"But . . ."

Chara Lee hung up the phone.

"Now, I must get the feast ready. This small town hasn't seen the likes of the social event I will put on."

Chara Lee strutted around town and ordered the best the town caterers could offer. She laughed at their pitiful, cheap prices.

"Ha! Is that all you could do?"

Mike was all of a sudden worried about Chara Lee's change of behavior. She was spending money left and right. He hoped she would slow down a bit.

"Where I come from, we bathe in money," Chara Lee said. "Now, be a good boy and run down to the store for some imported caviar. And I do mean imported!"

When Saturday arrived, Chara Lee was dressed in an elegant evening gown. She had on full-length, white gloves. When the doorbell rang, she went to the door and opened it with great snobbishness. Upon seeing her neighbors dressed in rags compared to her great clothes, she immediately had nothing but disdain for them.

"Do come in and see how the other side lives," she told them and walked off without even shaking their hands.

Soon, a limousine arrived with her college professors. They got out of the car with a beautiful red box.

"They're here. Everyone shut up. They have come to see me!" Chara Lee shouted, and everyone stopped their talking and looked as she went to the door.

"Chara Lee, Chara Lee," the professors said, "how good of you to invite us. We are truly pleased."

"Charmed, I'm sure," Chara Lee said, eagerly eyeing the red box.

"Now Chara Lee, we know you will be a little disappointed. . . " one of the professors said.

"Yes," another piped in, ". . . but we think you will remember this moment for the rest of your life."

"Instead of the one thousand dollars we originally said we would give you for your story. . . and after reading it, we must say that our memories were rather bad," another said.

". . . Oh yes, quite bad. We suddenly thought to ourselves that the award we should give you for such a story is . . . " another professor said.

"Is the Pudding Pie Award!" the professors said in unison.

"The . . . the Pudding Pie Award?" Chara Lee suddenly said and looked around the room at her guests who suddenly started to clap.

"Yes," one of the professors said, taking out a huge pudding pie from the red box. "Allow us to present you with the award!"

Chara Lee backed away, but it was too late, the professors took the pudding pie and threw it full force into her face.

"The Pudding Pie Award for the worst story ever submitted to an Ivy League university! Congratulations!"

Everyone clapped.

Even Mike.

The End

NO GHOST OF A CHANCE!

"I am Rebecca Sonnagan. I am the children's dead mother."

"What?"

"I would shake your hand, but I'm afraid I can't."

"I never! This is a joke. And a sick one at that!"

"Fine. If you want to try to shake my hand, go ahead," Rebecca said.

The woman reached for her hand, but, to her utter amazement, her hand went right through it.

"This . . . this . . ." she said in sputters.

"Please don't be afraid."

"This is the greatest thing I have seen in years!" the woman said with a clap. "How in the world did you manage to come back?"

"I found out that the exam had been postponed for a few more days."

"What?"

Peter walked into the kitchen.

"Hi, honey!" he said nonchalantly while waving his hand. "Aren't you suppose to be studying for an exam?"

Rebecca laughed.

"I never study for the exams! I just peek over the shoulder of the smartest student in the class and copy down all her answers. It's great to be invisible!"

Peter's face fell. He was wondering where all of his wife's morals had gone since her demise. Actually, her presence in the kitchen defied all that he had learned in Theology class. According to the Bible, she wasn't supposed to be here right now!

The maid, on the other hand, was busy boiling a kettle of hot water to fix two cups of tea. She pulled out some crumpets from her satchel.

"It's teatime!" she said gaily. "Come and sit down here, dear, and tell me all about it. How did you die?"

Peter and Rebecca sat down in the same chair at the same time. Rebecca fell right through the chair. Peter burst out laughing.

The maid failed to see the humor in this and attempted to help Rebecca up.

Unfortunately, her hands once again went right through her.

"Why is it that you go right through furniture, but you don't go through the floor?" she asked.

Rebecca shrugged her shoulders.

Screams from the bathroom indicated that the children's bath was over. Rebecca got up and started in their direction, but the maid told her to stop.

"I'll get them. I really don't think you can pick them up."

Rebecca watched her walk out of the kitchen. She turned to her ex-husband and started to cry.

"Why did it happen? What did I have to die so young?"

"Maybe you should think about going to whatever final abode you are destined to go to."

"But this is my destiny! Being a mother of five is my destiny."

"Was," Peter said.

Rebecca started to cry again.

"If I go now, I will never see you again," Rebecca said.

"I wouldn't say that," Peter said. "I have to die someday, too, you know."

"What if we don't end up in the same place?"

"I think you know the answer."

"Let me say goodbye to the children."

"Rebecca, they will be fine."

The maid walked in.

"The children are getting dressed. Will you be staying for dinner?"

"No, I'm afraid I must be going."

"Do come back often and have some tea with me," the maid said.

"She is leaving for her final resting place," Peter said.

"Well, let's do tea in about twenty or thirty years then," the maid said.

"Goodbye. I love you," Rebecca said to Peter.

"I love you, too, honey," Peter said and tried not to think about her leaving again for fear he would give her a tearful send off.

Rebecca began to vanish. Suddenly, her face began to take on a tormented, anguish expression.

"Oh no, I am burning! Burning!"

"Rebecca!" Peter screamed. "Come back!"

She stopped and winked.

"Just kidding."

The End

PUNISHMENT

He had known for years that his daughter had some sort of grudge against him. Somewhere between the ages of eight to ten, her relationship with her father had soured so that when the teenage years approached, she would often turn the other way when she saw her father and lock herself in her room.

Mr. Jones at first thought this sort of behavior was typical of girls as they grew up, but when it continued into her teens, he soon knew that there was something else that was preventing his daughter from loving him.

Finally, after years of patient waiting, Mr. Jones approached his daughter and told her to sit down since they needed to have a long talk.

"Why do we need to talk about anything?" his daughter said with a slight sneer.

"What have I done?" Mr. Jones said. "That you ignore me so much?"

"What have you done?" his daughter said and then began to laugh. "Oh c'mon. You cheated on mom! No man who cheats on his wife is worthy of my respect or love."

"Cheated? Cheated on your mother?" Mr. Jones said.

Suddenly, from within the kitchen, Mrs. Jones piped in, "Yes, you cheated on me! When we were playing a computer game, you made a deal with the computer players that you wouldn't do with me unless I gave you double money! You cheated! And you would do it again if you got the chance!" Mrs. Jones cackled.

Mr. Jones's daughter sat still.

"What else?" he asked his daughter.

"Well . . . uh . . . " his daughter said, "Mom said you are a lush."

"He sure is, honey!" Mrs. Jones cackled again. "He is one of the most luscious men I have ever met, and he is all mine!"

Mr. Jones's daughter started to squirm in her seat.

"What else?" Mr. Jones said, not believing this.

"Er," the daughter said, "Mom said your were dishonest."

Mrs. Jones walked in from the kitchen and held her arms wide apart.

"Your father is this honest," she said, "and I love you both this much!"

Beads of sweat appeared on Mr. Jones's daughter's forehead as she realized that she had seriously misjudged her father all these years. Five long years of animosity, over nothing!

"Well, Dad, I guess I misjudged you. I'm sorry for the way that I treated you all these years," she said.

Mr. Jones felt a huge weight lift from his shoulders. He felt that he should say something profound on such a solemn occasion as this.

"Er, there were two peanuts walking down the road and one was a salted," he ventured.

Mrs. Jones screamed with laughter and threw up her hands in delight.

"There is something that I didn't tell you, though," she chuckled and winked at Mr. Jones, "your father was a heavy hitter when he was younger."

Mr. Jones's daughter sat up in her chair with delight.

"Oh Dad! I didn't know that you were such a good baseball player when you were young!"

"Baseball?" Mr. Jones asked with a puzzled expression.

Mrs. Jones laughed again.

"Not baseball," she guffawed, "he lost control of the car and hit a bunch of things, including several pedestrians, before his car came to rest against a tree. Everyone settled out of court, though. That's how your father and I met."

Mr. Jones's face turned a beet red, and he was having trouble controlling himself. Their daughter was shocked to hear that her father had been in such a serious accident and didn't know what to think or say.

"I didn't realize hitting that machine over and over after I lost the game would cause such damage," Mr. Jones said. "It was the first automobile video game of its kind in the city as well. You were watching me play and introduced yourself to me."

"And the time you beat me?" Mrs. Jones reminded her husband.

"Which time?" Mr. Jones said. "Chess? Tennis? Bowling?"

The daughter looked at her mother and then her dad. She couldn't believe it. They talked incessantly in puns. There was never any hostility or other intent in their joking. It was just their way of having a good time.

"Uh . . . Mom," the daughter said, "are we having fish tonight?"

"Well, I haven't really thought about dinner tonight."

"How would you filet about mignon?" the daughter said and began to laugh.

Mr. And Mrs. Jones both stared at their daughter.

"Don't you mean 'feel' about it?" Mr. Jones said.

"Yes, it is not 'filet' about it," Mrs. Jones said with a laugh.

"Salmon said that if you want to have Sole, you should eat fish," their daughter continued.

"What are you talking about?" Mrs. Jones asked. "Don't you mean 'someone'? And I never heard that eating fish had anything to do with spirituality!"

"Mom, Dad! I'm getting a Haddock," the daughter said, exasperated.

"Then why don't you lie down, dear," Mr. Jones said.

Mr. Jones's daughter had enough of this.

"No! You don't understand. I'm making puns," the daughter said.

"Oh," Mrs. Jones said, "really?"

Mr. Jones's daughter didn't know what to say. Her father bent close to her ear and said:

"We either hang in there together, or we will hang separately."

He then sat back up in his chair.

"Now, that's a pun," he said to his frustrated daughter.

Mrs. Jones went back into the kitchen to make filet of salmon. Her daughter had said she was getting a Haddock so she would cook that later that week. She also remembered that her daughter had mentioned sole. She would cook that later also. Maybe, she thought, she could serve it with the puns her daughter was making.

"I do so hope those puns stay fresh," she said.

The End

FINAL THOUGHTS AND CONVERSATIONS OF THE TENANTS PRIOR TO THE COLLAPSE OF THEIR 25TH STORY BUILDING

Twenty-fifth Floor:
Man: You know, if you come out here and sit on the balcony, you can see a beautiful sunset.
Wife: Oh, honey, it is beautiful.
Man: You know. I have always considered myself lucky to have had you fall for me when we were young.
Wife: Believe me. I'd do it all over again if I had the chance.
Twenty-fourth Floor:
Phone rings:
(Voice on end of line): Hello, is this Chara Lee?
Chara Lee: Yes, it is.
(Voice on end of line, extremely excited): Congratulations. You have won a shopping spree to every store on Fifth Avenue in New York City.
Chara Lee: No!
(Voice on end of line): Yes! Come on down!
Twenty-third Floor:
Woman (home-schooling her son): What season comes after spring?

Son: Fall?

Woman: No. Guess again.

Twenty-second Floor:

Woman (watching television): This soap is a real downer.

Twenty-first Floor:

Man (finishing his book): I'll go down as the greatest novelist of all time.

Twentieth Floor:

Children have come down with something so their devoted mother has taken them to the doctor. They will be back in an hour.

Nineteenth Floor:

Gourmet Cook (drinking a cup of her homemade coffee) : I just love ground coffee.

Eighteenth Floor:

Man to friend: I lost my wife. I lost my job. I have just declared bankruptcy. How much further does a man have to go to reach rock bottom?

Seventeenth Floor:

Limbo Party: How low can you go?

Sixteenth Floor:

Woman (holding a test tube): The cure for Dropsy!

Fifteenth Floor:

Vacant. Rent was too high. Needs to come down.

Fourteenth Floor:

Young man to another young man: If you drop out of school, you might as well drop out of society all together.

Thirteenth Floor:

Sorry. The 13th floor has been undergoing extensive repairs. Multiple structural cracks.

Twelfth Floor:

Man to wife: (coughing) Honey, where are the cough drops?

Eleventh Floor:

Woman to friend: You really have to keep up with your housework, or else you will fall behind.

Tenth—First Floors:

I'm sorry, my wife was to finish these floors. She never did, and I can't wait for her to come along and finish. So, I am dropping the subject for now.

DAVID THE EASTER BUNNY

Joe's hands were shaking again. He was blacklisted. He was to have played Santa Claus at the annual Christmas party but he got drunk and passed out before he could perform. Now, he really wanted to be the Easter Bunny, but no one would have him.

David, on the other hand, was judged by the doctors to have slipped and hit his head in such a way as to cause a temporary lapse of sanity. He was forgiven for the way he had performed at the Christmas party, throwing his wife into the Christmas tree, throwing the presents at the little children, and pouring the water over the head of the company. He was now off everyone's list.

And he was now also the Easter Bunny!

David put on the bunny outfit with the cute, floppy ears and walked outside of his dressing room with a big basket of Easter eggs. He was really glad to be able to redeem himself socially. Suddenly, he ran straight into Joe who was waiting for him in the hall.

"Joe. What a pleasant surprise," David said.

Joe grabbed David.

"It wasn't my fault. It really wasn't. I was nervous," Joe said. "You just have to let me be the Easter Bunny!"

"Sorry, Joe, no can do," David said. "Now, if you will let me go, I will be going out into the nice Spring air to deliver Easter Eggs to all the children."

"No! I will not let you go!!!" Joe said and pulled on David's cute, fluffy little tail. David struggled to get away when, all of a sudden, the tail broke and David went hurdling forward straight into the door.

Cuckoo!

Joe ran away with the Easter Bunny's tail as David got up to his feet. He stood in a daze holding a basket of broken eggs. He looked around the hall for someone to please tell him who he was, but there was no one around. Right then, a little girl screamed out:

"Look! It's the Easter Bunny!"

David hopped down the hall and looked into the mirror. Sure enough! He was the Easter Bunny! He looked down and saw a little basket full of colorful, broken eggs.

"My basket!" he said. "And it's full of eggs!"

David hopped right out the building and threw an egg at the little girl who was waiting patiently for her egg.

"Merry Christmas!" David said. The little girl immediately started crying and ran off to find her mother.

"Hi honey!" David said to his wife who was helping with the Easter Brunch. "Wanna egg?"

"David? What are you doing out here so early," his wife said. "You aren't suppose to be out here now with that outfit on."

"I'm the Easter Bunny," David said. "I am delivering eggs to all the people in the world."

"What?" his wife said.

"Would you like an egg?" David said. "I think there are some in this potato salad."

David picked up the potato salad and poured it on his wife's head.

"ON MY LIST!" his wife said.

David hopped off to see if he could throw any more eggs. He quickly found many targets. A moving car. A security truck. A man walking his dog. The chairman of the company.

The chairman's car came to a screeching halt. The chairman rolled down his window.

"DAVID! You can't hop away from me!" he screamed after him. "YOU ARE ON MY LIST!!"

David quickly hopped into the bushes. He counted his eggs.

He had at least another two dozen. He decided he would hide them where everyone would be sure to find them. He would hide them in the road where all the cars and bicycles would be able to smash them to smithereens.

David was really happy. He was the Easter Bunny. It was a lifelong dream come true. It was a moment of self-actualization!

The End

NO TIME FOR SIESTA!

There was a rumor of it, but no one really knew for sure if it were true, but if it were true, that story was going to make the front page. The local newspaper sent a young reporter down to Mexico, to an obscure village, to try to find a young girl who was reputed to be a computer architectural wizard. The reporter was a computer buff himself so he was quite eager to take the trip. Besides, if the rumor were bogus, he would have a paid vacation and could go to the beach and swim and lie out in the sun.

When the reporter arrived in the village, he asked several people where the girl lived. No one seemed to know. He was quite downhearted. However, finally, an old woman, who was selling oranges, said that she thought she knew the girl he was speaking of and that no one ever understood a word of what she said or the inventions she was working on so they ignored her. The reporter nodded he understood, and the old woman pointed him down a narrow street. Overhead, rows of clothes hung on lines to dry. A few dogs scurried about. A shop owner or two sat outside their shops, looking around.

Finally, after an hour of what seemed to be wandering through an endless array of small narrow streets, the reporter finally came to a small apartment building where dirt and debris and garbage were strewn all over the place. The reporter walked into the building and found the girl's apartment. He knocked on the worn door, and it opened.

He came face to face with an unshaven man who was quite large, with black hair and a mustache and coal-black eyes.

"Yes?"

"My name is John Roberts. I am a reporter from America. I hear you have a daughter who designs computers?" John said.

"Yes. Please come in," the father said and shook his hand profusely. "Anita! Anita! You have a visitor."

The reporter was surprised to see a young, eight-year old girl come into the room.

"You design computers?" the reporter asked.

"Yes," said the girl in a small, feeble voice, "I have finished building my new machine. Would you care to see it?"

John nodded his head with growing excitement. The girl's father had his arm around his shoulder and was smiling broadly.

"My girl can do anything!" he said.

"I hope that what I have heard is true," the reporter said.

"Oh, more so, more so!" the father said and ushered the reporter into a damp and dark room in the back where paint was chipping off the walls. There, on a table, sat a small, white box with two slits.

"This is Pedro II," the girl said.

The reporter looked at the box and noticed it was the same as most of the computer boxes he had seen. It had what appeared to be a 1.44-Mb floppy drive and a CD-ROM player.

"What makes this machine so special?" he asked Anita.

"Well," Anita began, ". . . I know I shouldn't have made it look like a 1.44-Mb floppy disk drive, but I have developed a much similar storage device that holds over a trillion bytes of information."

"A trillion bytes? On a single floppy disk?" the reporter said writing this down.

"And we sell the disks for fifty cents," the father said gleaming.

"Fifty cents?" the reported asked.

"Is that too much to ask?" the little girl said.

The reporter assured her that she should try to sell the disks for a little more than fifty cents, but the girl felt guilty enough even suggesting fifty cents, so she left it at that price.

"Now, this machine also has an infinite hard drive."

"What?"

"It works on air. I suppose there are a finite number of electrons in the air, but I like to think of it as infinite because there is probably no way in the world for anyone to store that much information and hog up all the electrons in the air," Anita said.

"Yes, I agree," the reporter said, barely able to speak. "What else?"

"Siesta," the father said.

"Siesta?" the reporter asked.

Anita and her father went off to their small cots in the room and laid down. It was siesta time, and nothing anyone could do could stop them from taking their afternoon nap. The reporter had no choice but to lie down on the bare floor and take an afternoon snooze himself.

An hour passed. Then another. Then another. No one stirred. Finally, Anita and her father woke up, and Anita went into the kitchen to make supper. A little while later, the dinner was ready and the food smelled delicious. Anita walked over to the reporter and nudged him with her foot.

"Would you like some dinner?"

The reporter slowly woke up, opened his eyes, and looked around the room. What was he doing on the floor? This was no time for siesta! He had to get this story out. This machine would revolutionize the world!

"I have some black beans and goat meat," Anita said, looking down at his face.

The reporter got up and washed his face and then joined Anita and her father for a hearty repast of tantalizing Mexican food. It was the best he had eaten in a long time. He drank some beer since he was afraid of drinking the water. The father laughed and talked with the reporter for some time over the state of Mexican politics and village affairs. The reporter found this conversation quite enjoyable and wished to continue, but he knew that he needed to work on his story.

"I'm sorry," the reporter said, "but I would like to ask you a few more questions about your computer."

"Sure! What else would you like to know?" the father said.

"How fast does the machine go?" the reporter said.

"As fast as an electron vibrates," Anita said.

"Oh," the reporter said and wrote that down. He then put his paper down and asked whether he could have some more beer and more beans and goat.

"Certainly!" the father said, and Anita got up with a smile and ran to the kitchen. She was glad someone liked her cooking. Her mother would have been proud of her.

"One day. . . " the father said, "Anita will make someone a fine wife!"

"If she cooks like this!" John said.

"You know, if you stay here and help me farm my land," the father said. "In seven years, you can marry my daughter."

"It's a deal!" the reporter said, and the two men shook heartily.

The next seven years seemed but a day, as John Roberts worked alongside Anita's father, Pedro. The harvest was always adequate to help feed the family, and Anita was always able to take whatever was harvested and make a mighty fine meal. Anita grew lovelier every year, and finally, the day for betrothal arrived.

"I want to wear Mother's wedding gown," Anita told her father, and he let out a little cry.

"She would be so proud," Pedro said and bent down and kissed his daughter.

John was happier than he had ever been. He couldn't wait to marry Anita. He put on his suit with great care, making himself look the best that he could to impress his new bride. She was so lovely. Nothing could ruin this occasion.

During the wedding ceremony, John held Anita tenderly. He made sure she was well taken care of and had enough to eat and drink.

The neighbors were all wishing them the best of everything, and right when it looked like it couldn't get any better, the town Maruichi band came marching in playing a rousing song. Everyone got up to sing and dance. Suddenly, right when the song was at its highest pitch and the people were singing and dancing at their highest point of ecstasy, John dropped his bottle of beer and looked as if he had seen a ghost.

"My story! How could I have forgotten it?" he said. "Anita? Do you remember the machine that you built years ago?"

"The one I made when I was a little child?" Anita said.

"Yes," John said.

"You are so funny," Anita said and began to laugh. "That was just a made-up machine. A child's toy."

"What?" John said and then began to laugh.

"I used to create machines all the time," Anita said, "but they were just imaginary toys."

"You silly girl," John said and took her in her arms and kissed her. "But, if it weren't for your vivid imagination, I would never have met you."

"And if it weren't for my cooking, you would never have married me," Anita said.

They both laughed and held each other tight and looked over the crowd and laughed again. And, while they were doing this, Anita made a mental note to bury the machine she had hidden under the bed. Life was too short, she thought, to have it spoiled with technology.

The End

THE PERFECT MOTHER—A SHORT, SHORT SUMMARY OF PERFECTION

She was the perfect mother. Sacrificially raising two twin daughters on her own, catering to their needs without a thought of herself, working two jobs and managing to find time for their school events, helping them with their schoolwork, crying with them and laughing with them.

Veronica was held up as an example by others in the community of what true motherhood was all about. She was highly sought after for her expertise on how to manage the affairs of a very busy life. All the women's groups looked to her as the fulfilled woman, and she even received an award or two.

And her daughters? Her daughters were raised as model children. They did excellent in school. They were polite. And when they became teenagers, they were responsible and didn't fall for some guy just because he was good-looking and a jock and had lots of money and wanted her to be his for the rest of his life until some other girl came along.

And when it came time for graduation and time to go to college, Veronica told her daughters that money was no object. So, when they were both accepted to Harvard, at an exorbitant tuition a year, Veronica told her daughters that it was no problem.

The town was a buzz. With her jobs? How could she have saved so much money?

So Veronica did the right thing for her daughters. She walked into the local police station and confessed that she was a non-custodial parent and had kidnapped her twin daughters years ago to keep them from their rich father who she thought would not be a good choice since he was so rich and would surely spoil them even though he loved them very much.

When the girl's father heard that his babies had been found, he was so happy. He was also tickled pink that they were going to his alma matter and all too glad to pay the cost. Nothing was too good for his girls!

And Veronica went to jail. Before she did, she kissed her daughters and cried with them. She was so very proud of how they had turned out and would love to receive pictures of them and their families-to-be in the future while she served out her sentence.

Veronica was indeed the model of motherhood. She sacrificed everything for her daughters, even her very life, so that they would continue on the road to success. She was indeed an example of sacrificial love and would often think of them in prison.

The End

THE LOVE BIRDS

Brown-haired Thomas looked out the window at the freshly mowed grass and the spring flowers sprayed across the lawn like a rainbow egg dropped from a great height that cracked and splattered its multitudes of colors. He glanced at his reflection in the mirror and smiled. His violet polo shirt with delicate white mother of pearl buttons and his suede pants with suspenders made him ever so attractive. The blue of his eyes complemented his outfit with the finest complement known to humankind.

And yet, there was another reflection. Not one in the mirror. No, this reflection was deep in his heart. It was a reflection of utter, deep, so very deep love. The love that no man could have ever known. Only Thomas, and Thomas alone, could feel such a love for such a reflection.

And the reflection's name was Annette.

Thomas wanted a sandwich, and, he wanted one right now! So Thomas made his way into his kitchen looking for something to eat, and real fast. He was famished! And thirsty too!

First, he found the mustard, mayonnaise, lettuce, pickles, tons of meat stuff, and a lot of different types of bread. He was going to make himself a hero sandwich, to honor his war torn love relationship with Annette.

Quote the hero sandwich: "Nevermore!"

They say that men who drink heavily have profound, abysmal psychological problems, to say the least. Even though it was only a few glasses of milk to go with his sandwich, Thomas was still unable to quench the bottomless yearning he had for his lovely Annette, and yet he continued to pour out glass after glass of milk to quench his thirst—besides, the hero sandwich had stale bread which made him gag every other second. Outside of that, however, the sandwich was pretty good.

Thomas also needed a good morning stretch. He held onto the kitchen cabinet and did some deep knee bends. He then held his hands up high and tried to touch his 15-foot ceiling.

"Stretch!" He said. "I must stretch those arms."

And then, there was a good show on TV that morning. A favorite Saturday morning cartoon that he enjoyed watching. One that would help him forget about his aching love for Annette. However, during watching, Thomas suddenly remembered he had left the phone off the hook the night before so as not to be disturbed by Annette calling him late at night.

Annette woke up to the sound of birds chirping on her windowsill and the bright sunlight streaming through her window. The curtains fluttered in a gentle breeze that blew into her room and across her face. She smiled and stretched her arms over her head and then snuggled one more time in the billows of down feathers and eyelet lace that covered her bed. She got up and examined herself in the mirror. She saw a beautiful girl with violet-blue eyes framed by long wavy black hair. She decided to take a bubble bath.

The water was running in the bathtub when the phone rang. Annette ran to get it, hoping it was Thomas. She had tried to call him several times during the night, but it was always busy. Still, she never wondered who he might be talking to at those times or if he took the phone off the hook and why. Her mother's cheery voice greeted her on the phone.

"Hello, Annette, my darling," she said, "this is your wake-up call. How are you this morning, sweetie-pie?"

"Just fine, mother," Annette answered disappointedly. "What do you want?"

"How could you think such a thing," the mother replied in a huff. "All I wanted was to hear the sound of my one and only daughter's voice this morning and brighten up her day a little. But, if you really want to know what I want…well, I want my daughter to meet a nice, wonderful man and settle down, instead of spending her whole life snuggling in billows of down feathers and eyelet lace and taking bubble baths in billows of bubbles and eyelet lace towels. . . ."

"Don't have a cow, dude," Annette replied and hung up the phone.

When Annette got back to the bathtub, the water and the bubbles were pouring out of the bathtub and onto the bathroom floor. Annette had to use every towel in the house to mop up the floor, leaving nothing but a tiny towel for herself. She didn't feel at all refreshed after her bubble bath and not at all dry. Her beautiful long black hair hung down her shoulders like many strips of dirty black rags. In fact, if she had some feathers in her hair, she would have looked like someone who had been tarred and feathered. Suddenly, she slipped on a bar of soap.

"Grrr." Annette said.

Thomas decided to play a practical joke on Annette's mother. Besides, he thought, she would be his mother-in-law one-day.

He ran to the phone and dialed Mrs. Jones's number.

"Hello," a rather curt voice said, almost as if someone she dearly loved had hit her with a ton of bricks, or rather, a collapsing room full of bath water for some odd reason.

Thomas, trying his best not to laugh, suddenly couldn't help himself.

"Ha, ha, ha!" He guffawed with tears rolling down his cheeks.

"Who is this?" Mrs. Jones demanded.

Thomas quickly hung up, laughing hysterically.

He then took the phone off the hook again.

"Saturday morning cartoon not over," he said in a monotone voice.

Annette decided to stick some feathers in her hair from her down comforter and dress up in a suede Indian dress and moccasins. Wouldn't Thomas be pleased at the new Annette!

"Ugh," Annette practiced in the mirror with an ugly scowl on her face, "How, me wanna wampum. Me heap pretty squaw."

Then, Annette began dancing around her bedroom, whooping and howling in what looked like an Indian war dance. She danced all the way downstairs into the kitchen and grabbed a knife from the drawer.

"Me go hunting for chow," Annette grunted.

Annette creeped and crawled through the bushes in the neighborhood, looking for game.

Unfortunately, wild game was quite rare in the posh neighborhood of Beverly Hills. The only wild things there were the people and the parties. She slowly made her way to Thomas's house and started peering through all the windows.

"This some strange teepee," she pondered, "Needum big fire stick to get in here!"

Annette, now calling herself "Girl with Tar Hair" stalked off looking for her fire stick.

Thomas plugged the phone back into the wall now that his morning cartoon feast was consumed. The rich pâté he had succored was the most delightful of all of his 34 years. But, it was nothing as rich as Annette. She was a regale of the purist sophist refineries all wrapped into one.

The phone rang.

"Annette?" Thomas said frantically with great hope, but alas, it was not Annette, but Annette's mother.

"Is your refrigerator running?" She asked, trying her best to mask her voice.

"Hold on, I'll go check," Thomas said and put her on hold.

While in the kitchen, Thomas looked outside at the beautiful spring day. The morning air was refreshing. He even heard some birds chirping gaily on the cherry tree with its beautiful, pink blossoms.

While Annette was creeping through the underbrush, she rammed her pretty little feathered head into a tree.

"Ouch," she yelled, rubbing the top of her head, "What happened?"

She stared at her clothing and hair in horror.

"What are these feathers doing in my hair and why am I wearing an Indian costume," she screamed. Annette quickly ran all the way home to fix herself before any of the neighbors—or worse, Thomas—saw her.

Muddy and dirty from all the crawling she had done as "Girl with Tar Hair," Annette decided to take another luxurious bubble bath. This time, no annoying phone call from her mother interrupted. Annette slipped into the water and lay back with a sigh.

Annette stared up at the ceiling and thought about the first time she saw Thomas. It was a beautiful spring day like this one. Annette was taking a bubble bath when she heard the doorbell ring. A little annoyed but curious, Annette slipped a billowy bathrobe trimmed with eyelet lace and answered the door. A peculiar man stood on her front porch. His ugliness was a sharp contrast to her beauty. He had on a strange pair of glasses, and his buckteeth made him look like the Easter Bunny.

"What's up?" He asked and stuck his foot in the door, "Hey, my little chickadee, I'm here to sell you some eggs. Want 5 dozen or so?"

"Hop right on out of here, Peter Rabbit," Annette answered curtly, "or I'll make a rabbit stew out of you."

Suddenly, an ambulance attendant showed up behind the strange man and grabbed him.

"Sorry, miss," he said apologetically, "We were taking him to the hospital when he jumped out of the back of the truck. Hope he hasn't scared you or bothered you."

Annette smiled warmly at the attendant who was the handsomest thing she had ever seen.

"Any more like you at home or did they break the mold when you were born," she teased.

"Just me and my brother Thomas," the ambulance attendant replied with a wink.

Annette and Terence, the ambulance attendant, dated for several months before she was asked to come over to his house for dinner and to meet his family. When she rang the doorbell, the most gorgeous man she had ever seen since Terence opened the door. "Any more like you at home or did they break the mold when you were born," she teased.

"Just me and my brother Terence," the gorgeous man replied with a wink.

Annette was in love!

Thomas walked outside and breathed the fresh air. He looked down and saw his tulip bulbs popping up with the most beautiful bulbs he had ever seen. There were red ones, blue ones, purple ones, and white ones. He counted each and every one. He was so very proud of his tulip collection. He knew that Annette loved tulips, so he gathered a whole bunch of them and took them back into the house. He tenderly arranged them in green cellophane paper, and put them in a flower box. These would be for Annette and nobody else. He then took the box and made a mad dash out to the street when he suddenly remembered that he had someone on hold. He would apologize later.

He ran as fast as his legs would carry him to Annette's house. However, he had forgotten to bring the car to pick her up. He quickly ran back to get the car keys. Once he had them, he quickly ran and jumped into the car.

Thomas loved his car almost as much as he loved Annette, if not even more. He gunned the engine and raced out of the driveway.

Halfway to Annette's house, Thomas stopped with a screech of tires.

"I forgot the flowers!" he said.

He turned around and raced home. He retrieved the flowers that laid on the freshly mowed lawn next to a broken tulip that he had stepped on while trying to get the keys to the car of his dreams.

He got back into his car and raced back to Annette's house.

Mrs. Jones was still patiently waiting for Thomas to come back and tell her that his refrigerator was running so she could finish her prank. However, it was becoming such a bore to wait.

The joke was turning into a great, big bore.

And this story (much like this collection of short stories) was becoming a great, big bore. A big, fat bore.

The End

APPENDIX

Every appendix should have a deep saying. Something that is profound. Hence:

What is humor?

Is it something you can put under a microscope and dissect, looking for its components? Many people ask this when they try and write a humorous short story. Unfortunately, their humor falls short on many occasions due to the following:

1. Clichés—How many times do we hear the same thing over and over and over again until it is no longer funny? This is television comedy. Recycled garbage, served on a different colored platter, but formula, stock, and boring all the same. Not original. Just something to pass the time of day and a pat on the back for the television actors and actresses stuck in such a mindless career.

2. Clichés—Same old stuff, over and over and over again. Never funny after a few times, but people keep on using it to sound clever. The younger generation uses it to sound cool but are too ignorant to realize that the older generation has already heard it and are bored to tears. This is why television comedy works. They target the younger generation.

3. Clichés—Like a broken record. Never stopping. Click. Click.. Never stopping. Click. Click . . .

4. How to put humor into your stories

Sometimes, you should add a little humor to help your readers have a good laugh. Unfortunately, many of us are not high-paid Hollywood comedians nor have a great sense of humor. Let's look at a scene:

"Hello," the man said. "What is your name?"
"Cuckoo," the man said.

Is this funny? No, not really. It is actually quite trite. Let's make it more interesting:

"Hello," the man said. "What is your name?"
At that very moment, a sudden wind blew a large metallic object right on the visitor's head.
"Cuckoo," the man said.

Is this funny? Well, you do have something hit the man on the head. Depending on your sense of humor, this is either funny or tragic. The man is obviously not named "Cuckoo." It is just an expression of total insanity before he collapses to the floor.

Okay, let's delay the man saying "Cuckoo." In fact, let's make him say the word with a pause between syllables.

"Hello," the man said. "What is your name?"
At that very moment, a sudden wind blew a large, metallic object right on the visitor's head.
"Cu . . . " the man said.
"Pleased to meet you Mr. Cu," the man said.
". . . Ckoo," the man said.
"Yes, Mr. Cu," the man said. "Pleased to meet you."

Do you see the humor? There is a play on words. The man has said "Cuckoo" in such a way as to make the other man think he is saying his name twice. But, could it be funnier? Let's try delaying the other man's sentences.

> "Hello," the man said. "What is . . . "
> At that very moment, a sudden wind blew a large, metallic object right on their heads.
> "Name?" the man said.
> "Cu . . . " the visitor said.
> "Cu . . . "the man said.
> ". . . Ckoo." the visitor said.
> ". . . Ckoo." the man said.

Isn't this a little more original?

You need to avoid the obvious when it comes to humor. Make your reader feel like he is reading something that he has never seen before and you may get a laugh.

Okay, finally, get rid of superfluous sentences and tighten up the scene, and you'll be done.

> "Cu . . ." the man said.
> ". . . Ckoo," the visitor said.

See! A comic gem.

Printed in the United States
3019